Loving Two

Women

By

Matthew Lutostanski

I dedicate this book to my parents, Misiu and Tatus,
who steered me with their love in my formative years.
And to my beautiful children and grand-children
who rock my world.

CONTENTS

CHAPTER 1

She licked the envelope flap and sealed it. Finally. She carried the letter to the local Post Office. She had to pay extra for the overseas cost of stamps. The lady behind the counter took the letter and tossed it into a bin behind her. Gone. The letter was on its way to change his life.

It was as early as 6am and already a bright, fresh spring morning... All was still except the birds were chirping in the trees. Always looking for any morsels that happened to be emerging from the earth in abundance. Just around the back of the house, the grey squirrels had already gathered for their daily breakfast, in the form of nuts laid on by Maria. It was a daily routine which they followed and by now all of them were pretty tame, feeding from Maria's hands. The younger ones were still unsure but they still advanced, trusting in the example set by the older squirrels.

The postman was already coming down the long and crunchy drive carrying his usual hefty sack ready to deliver mail for the large house.

Tadeusz and Maria had lived at this house in Bournemouth for over 15 years. It was a small hotel with around 25 rooms, originally built for the Mayor of Bournemouth back in the 1890s. Typically Victorian in style, it was positioned close to Meryck Park golf course and only a brisk walk from the beach. The hotel rooms were all of a decent size and the main hall had a large sweeping staircase up to the first floor. With a huge chandelier hanging centrally, looming over the bannister. Almost all the wood was dark original mahogany. The hotel had a musty smell, inevitable for such an old property. But Maria kept it spotless and the wood was polished to a mirror reflection.

Tadeusz, in his late 50's, was a tall man, strongly built. He always sported a shirt and tie, even at weekends, in that old-fashioned way. Very much a traditionalist who preferred proper form every time, rather than carefree and lax attitudes. He hated having much to do with people, which was odd, as he and Maria owned a hotel in the service industry. Tadeusz liked his own time and enjoyed pottering, away from anybody else. Maria, was in stark contrast, in that she was short and slim but full of energy. With an endless resolve to make all things right and to deal with people from all walks of life. Everybody loved Maria as she was always ready to stop and share a few words or indulge in any amount of local gossip. But she did not give much away about herself, nor about her husband Tadeusz. She kept family matters secret and always had done so.

Tadeusz was an early riser. So, he usually went down to meet the postman and collect the mail, consisting mostly of bills and a few holiday bookings. He spent a few moments chatting to the postman about the weather and the usual politics about which he loved to share his thoughts.

He would then join his beloved Maria in the large kitchen at the back of the house, for their breakfast of black coffee, a little cereal and then the cigarettes. Always the cigarettes.

They sat and chatted amiably, talking about the new guests who were due to arrive that morning. They discussed the need to get all the beds changed and made up. Maria mentioned that she needed to talk to Joanna the maid again, to ensure that she did her job properly. Recently she had been slacking probably because she was not paid a decent rate and so she delivered pretty much to the level of her poor pay. Maria was already grabbing a second cup of black coffee and she hurried off to supervise the Saturday morning switch of laundry in all the rooms.

Tadeusz went to his favourite old Victorian desk to settle in for a couple of hours with the bookings and the bills. He liked to do the bookwork as it gave him the opportunity to stay away from the details of running the hotel. He left all the daily chores to his Maria, who certainly knew how to run the place.

Tadeusz flicked through the envelopes and then spotted the foreign letter. But not so foreign, as it was stamped from Poland. And Tadeusz and Maria were both Polish, having come to England after the war with their only son, Maciek.

Tadeusz stared at the envelope. He knew it was

4

not from his family as he couldn't recognise the handwriting. He was intrigued. Slowly he turned it over to see if the sender had recorded their name on the back of the envelope. But there was nothing there. He peeled back the flap to find a letter with a few pages. Four in fact.

He opened the pages and began to read. Very quickly his mouth went dry. He felt his head go hot, as if in a fever. His hand was shaking as he got past the first few paragraphs.

My darling Tadeusz,

At last I have found you. I thought you were dead. Friends had told me that you died in Siberia. I lived in unbelievable shock when you were first taken. I spent time with your parents who also believed that you had perished. They were both totally broken having lost first your beloved brother, Henryk, to the Germans in Auschwitz and then you to camps in Siberia. Both in just a matter of weeks.

I spent over four years in a deep depression, thinking only about you and how harsh it was that I had not even had the chance to see you before you were taken. To stroke your face. To see your radiant smile. To hug you closely to my body. To feel your love and warmth. To feel the strength and safety of your arms around me. Oh, how many times I tried to recapture those moments we shared together. Times when all was good in our lives. We were only weeks from our wedding. How was it possible to have it all stolen in just one night? And then to lose you forever? How was I supposed to cope with that pain in my heart and in my soul?

The tragedy surrounding our beloved Polska was a small part of my grief. All I could think about was what might have been. What we had and then had no longer. Just snatched from us both before we could even start our lives.

I spent years grieving for you. And then one day last month, I was told by a family friend that you were still alive and well in England?!!! I almost fainted. I felt physically sick with excitement and with sadness, both at the same time. Excitement that perhaps I could speak to you again and sadness that over 35 years had passed, and our love had been extinguished by fate. When I was first told I literally stumbled. I simply could not stand. I spent many days considering what I should do. I could not sleep for many nights. But nothing was ever going to stop me finding you and speaking to you, even if only one last time.

Darling Tadeusz, I know nothing of your life, of your new

loves or even if you have any children. All I know is where you live and that we have lost so many years together.

I should tell you a little about me first. After the war, I finally met another solicitor in Warsaw. He pursued me but I was less than convinced. In my heart the love we had could never be replaced. But my mother pushed me. She told me that some compromise would be of value and that I would grow to love this man. His name is Witold. He is a really fine person with wonderful values. I did grow to love him. We married and over the years I had 5 sons. An enormous family! None of it was planned that way but we carried on. We were good Catholics, so we tried to practice birth control but with little success. I absolutely love all of my sons. We live a good life as I am now a Judge in Poland and so is Witold.

I did not tell him about you. I am barely able to think even when writing this letter. I feel so very private about us. About what we had. I was so young and so in love with you. The world was at our feet. And then you died. Or so I was told?? Can you even begin to imagine how I felt? Or have you forgotten about me? Have the years and your life moved you on? Am I wrong to have written to you? I will not re-read this letter as it was written from the bottom of my heart. I did not want to think too much. Nor consider any consequences. I just wanted to speak to you again. To hear your voice again. I am terrified that this letter might be a mistake. You might throw it to one side and then what will I do? How will I deal with the knowledge that you are still alive but not available, my darling Tadeusz? By now this letter will have gripped your very soul or you will be thinking of how to pass it by. I no longer know you. I don't know who you are as you are. I only know the handsome young man with whom I graduated at University and agreed to marry with all my body and soul. You were pure. You were so clever. And now I trust in those beliefs. You will know what to do and what to say.

I should tell you, although am sure you know, that both your parents died in the bombing of Warsaw. I had moved away two years after you had been taken and lost contact with your parents. I do not think either of us could contemplate, any further, the possibility of your survival. Especially as all reports coming from Siberia stated that most Polish officers had died of malnutrition or been executed. None of us was able to think about that anymore.

I have now decided that just knowing you are alive is enough. Knowing that the man I cherished and adored is still in my world. The next step is up to you, my darling Tadeusz.

All my deepest love, Ella.

Tadeusz dropped the letter on the floor. His head was spinning and heart racing. Nothing but nothing could have prepared him for this letter. He could not even start to gather his thoughts. What did he think? What did he know? What were his emotions telling him? What about Maria – if she walked in? Should he tell her or keep it a secret – even for a little while? Spinning back to him... his emotions? What did he really think? What Ella had said... Her words were so beautiful and they made deep sense. But who was she? Where did she come from? Was he really engaged to be married to Ella? He couldn't breathe properly.

Tadeusz suffered from high blood pressure, so he was not surprised that his pulse was racing. But there was nothing that could calm him. He picked up the letter and hid it in his bottom drawer. He lay down on the bed to gather himself. He had laid on the bed for only 10 minutes when Maria walked in and immediately said: 'Tadeusz, are you OK? You look white. Shall I call the doctor? Did you take your tablets?'

Tadeusz nodded slowly. His reply was not clear.

He stuttered: 'I think… I think I had a small attack or something…' He had suffered from palpitations before, so he opted for that as his excuse.

Maria went to the phone and called the doctor despite his protestations. Tadeusz was slightly relieved as it gave him a chance to mask his shock. He was still reeling from the letter and its impact on his head and his heart. And then the guilt kicked in. *What about my beloved Maria? The woman with whom I have spent my whole life?*

He rolled over on his side to hide his face, pretending that it felt better if the body weight was not pressing on his heart. He closed his eyes and waited for the doctor.

Maria was really concerned. She had not seen Tadeusz in this state since his small attack some six years before. She asked: 'Are you OK? Do want a tea or glass of water? What about your tablets – are you sure you took them this morning?'

Tadeusz shook his head side to side. 'No thanks. I feel slightly sick. But yes, I did take my tablets.'

'Good,' she murmured.

Maria knew that the tablets were designed for

exactly this kind of mild heart tremor. But she wanted the doctor to confirm her thoughts.

The doctor arrived a little after 12 noon. He knew Tadeusz's medical condition and all about his blood pressure. They had sometimes exchanged the usual gags about 'pressures from the wife', although this banter mostly came from Tadeusz who liked a joke at the expense of his Maria.

The doctor was a good friend to both of them and had often popped by for an evening drink to chat about politics with Tadeusz. It was a common subject they both enjoyed discussing together.

After his brief examination, he concluded that there was nothing inherently wrong. Nothing visible at least. He asked Tadeusz a few more cursory questions, but it was clear to him that perhaps he should not have been called out to this patient. He packed his medical bag and said his goodbyes. Maria called after him asking if they owed him anything.

The doctor replied tersely as he got into his car: 'My office will let you know. Good morning, Maria.'

Maria returned to Tadeusz and sat on the bed.

'Are you alright, my darling? What can I get you?

Shall I pop and get you the newspaper so you can read in bed and rest?' Maria was already making the bed ready for her Tadeusz.

But he was not happy. His Maria was fussing around him. Yes, it was nice to be loved and looked after, but equally he knew that this was all a sham. Caused by the impact of the extraordinary letter he had just received. He tried to resurrect the contents of the letter into his head but could not. It was all still a blur. Slightly undefined. But he knew that his Ella had found him and now contacted him. But why was she his Ella? Surely, he should know that his life had indeed moved on. He had spent many loving years with his Maria and so enjoyed their many years together. His thoughts darted back and forth while Maria tried to push pillows behind his neck and shoulders.

'There. You should sit up a little. And catch your breath. Stay calm and I'm sure it will be better in an hour or two.'

'Yes,' he replied. 'You're right. I just need a couple of hours of rest and maybe a little nap.'

Maria nodded agreement and left him with the curtains closed. She stood by the door and said: 'Take off your tie, Tadeusz. Undo your top button, for goodness' sake!'

Tadeusz had always been a traditionalist. He wore a shirt tie and jacket no matter what the weather or what he was doing during the day. Even when he wore his DIY overalls to do his little jobs around the hotel grounds, even then his shirt and tie were perfectly in place. He allowed himself a small change for weekends when he wore a checked country shirt with tie.

Maria had gone. Tadeusz got up quietly and reached into the bottom drawer of his old desk. He withdrew the letter and settled back into bed to read it again.

The impact on re-reading was almost as strong as the first reading. It really didn't make much sense as he had long ago given up on his previous life back in Poland. The war had really damaged his psyche. He had pretty much decided that his parents and Ella were dead, having been killed during the war. He had asked a few of his contacts towards the end of the war, but he was told repeatedly that his old house was destroyed by German bombs. And nobody was left. So, his heart, heavy with the sadness of his colossal loss, decided to move on. It was not as if he was going anywhere new, as there was nothing new on his horizon. But he had given up any notion of survival of his parents or Ella.

CHAPTER 2

Maria and Tadeusz's journeys were the same as for so many post-war refugees coming to the UK. Tadeusz originated from an established Polish family, whose land was situated in the northern part of Poland, in a small hamlet. His father Marian had been a First Polish Consul representing the Polish Government in Russia. Tadeusz was born in July 1916 in Moscow. This was the period when Tsar Nicholas was still in power in Russia at the beginning of the First World War. As diplomats, Tadeusz's parents would often attend the court of the Romanovs and enjoy the remarkable opulence and wealth those gatherings provided. Nobody realised at the time, but the growing desperation of the masses and the revolution was not far away. An extraordinary period in Europe's history as the world watched the transition of power from the Royal Throne of the 300-year-old Romanov Tsars to the establishment of Communism by the poverty-stricken people who had had enough oppressive Tsarist rule. By the end of the war, in 1918, the Romanov empire had finally collapsed, and the Tsar and his family had been executed.

Marian and his wife Marta returned to Warsaw in 1918 with their two sons, Henryk, and Tadeusz. Marian was a qualified chemist, so he opened a chemist store in central Warsaw. Life was good during the twenties. Both sons were studying law in Wilno – a beautiful city which, after the war, became Vilnius as part of the recovered country of Lithuania. Henryk, the eldest son, was considered the bad apple who liked to gamble and party at nights. Yet despite the lingering concerns about Henryk's lifestyle, the whole family lived a prosperous life enjoying all the success generated after the harrowing First World War.

Then, in 1929 the first wave of the dramatically damaging recession hit Europe. The world's investments crashed without hope. The stock markets collapsed. Many people lost their entire life's wealth and savings. The Deutschmark in Germany had lost its value. People were wheeling barrow loads of paper money to pay for the simplest of domestic goods. There was a serious depression in Europe in the early thirties and Germany suffered particularly badly with their shattered economy. And that's how the sinister growth of Nazism emerged. Adolf Hitler had built a powerful and dominant party. The Germans were thrilled to listen to him, as they believed in his promises and propaganda about the growing strength of the German people. The Germans had always believed in the pride of their nation. Always held a sense of supremacy that still exists in Europe, even today. Right-wing sentiments had constantly stalked the corridors of power in Germany, well past the Second World War, into the last decades of the 20th century.

Tadeusz, now a recently qualified solicitor in 1939, was engaged to be married to Ella, his beautiful girlfriend, who had also recently qualified in law. They had met and fallen in love when they were both studying law at Vilnius University.

Ella came from a family of legal people in that both her father was a judge and her older brother a barrister. So, when Tadeusz became so close to Ella he was welcomed with open arms into her family. Tadeusz and Ella spent as much time together as they could manage between studies. They travelled to the Tatra mountains in the summer. To hike. To take long romantic walks. To share evenings by the open fire. Yet in those more traditional times they did not share a bed. They were saving themselves for marriage. So, their love was perfect. They never had opportunities to share even the smallest cross word. They were so happy and all their friends and both families were thrilled for them. They made plans to buy a house on the banks of the Vistula River running through central Warszawa. They talked of children they would have and even teased each other with their personal favourite names for these children of the future.

So, the plans had been firmly laid. The wedding date was fixed. Invitations had been sent out. It was going to be a grand affair in the beautiful old square in the middle of Warsaw. They planned to have huge marquees across the square, something often done in the old square for special weddings.

As their special day approached so did Hitler with his aggressive plans to dominate Europe. So, in the fateful late summer of 1939, he declared war on Poland. Hitler had already established a secret pact with Stalin to divide and share Poland's land, thereby annihilating the Polish Kingdom from the maps of Europe. September 1939 and the following months were a time of disintegration of all that bore the name of Poland. The state ceased to exist, the army was defeated, personal and family safety did not exist, and the future was grim and uncertain. The same fate was shared by those who crossed the borders of Poland to fight for their country abroad.

The Poles took up arms, but they were not in any state of readiness for war. Whereas the Germans had been building their armies for months, precisely for this first strike. Poland was overrun from the west by the Nazis and also destroyed by Stalin's Red Army from the east. The first years of the war were horrifying. The Russians, determined to crush any rebellion from the Poles, decided that the best strategy was to capture and imprison the "intelligentsia" in

Poland. It meant gathering both educated Poles and army officers. Most were taken to northern Siberia, where they were thrown into concentration camps. The conditions were desperately bleak. Many of the Poles died of either starvation or from the sheer effects of sub-zero temperatures.

Undeniably, the strong support of the Soviets was an important element in the German victory over Poland and on the western front. The Soviets invaded the eastern part of Poland on 17th September 1939, occupied it and systematically persecuted and arrested the people living there. 180,000 Polish troops in this area were interned and later they were imprisoned in concentration camps. Thousands of interned officers were moved to Kozielsk, Ostaszkow, Starobielsk and Katyn where a large number of them were executed by a single bullet in the back of the head. Hundreds of thousands of Poles – men, women and children – were deported by rail, in cattle trucks, to remote parts of the Soviet Union and condemned to hard labour, hunger and early death.

Marian and Marta, who believed that they still held some political influence, were trying to protect their sons in Warsaw by using diplomatic favours, but with little success. Henryk the eldest son, was one of the first prisoners to be taken by the Germans and he arrived in 1940, in the notorious new concentration camp called Auschwitz. Henryk was there for only 10 months. He perished there in the ovens in October 1941, less than one year after arriving at Auschwitz. The camp was originally designed to take political prisoners, mostly Poles, but then very quickly they were followed by Jews gathered from all over Europe. By late 1941, the extermination plans for the Jewish population in Europe, were in full flow. The Germans were building concentration camps all over Poland.

Back in Warsaw the Russians were now established in the city. Destruction of the key buildings was their priority. And to capture officers and any people of higher education. Their thinking was to destroy any potential leadership that might strive to create a revolution. Tadeusz was taken, in the middle of the night, to a concentration camp in Siberia. He was not even allowed to say goodbye to his parents. Tadeusz was heart-broken, as he was due to be married only weeks later. He could not send any message to his beloved fiancée, Ella. He and many fellow officers were spirited away in the direction of north of Murmansk some 1,600 miles into northern Russia. Murmansk is the largest city in the world above the Arctic Circle, and it is an established port for Russian military ships and submarines. The journey took weeks and little food was made available to the prisoners. By now, Tadeusz now knew that he would never see his Ella or his parents again. If he did survive, then it would probably be into a different life and a new world. But that thought was not a realistic option and his heart was not optimistic. All seemed lost.

In the camps, starvation and vitamin deficiency were the norm. Multiple deaths an everyday occurrence. The light days in Murmansk lasted six months and the other six months were in virtual darkness. The damp wooden huts were enveloped in a really harsh and brutal environment. Tadeusz was thrown into Hut 32 with some of his closest friends in Warszawa. Life was desperate in the first few months, as they tried to cope with the bitter cold, the lack of food and the terrible sleeping conditions on wooden benches with no mattresses. They had only recently all lived decent lives, mostly with parents and families. How quickly were those memories snatched from them.

In 1941, Hitler's ambitions were expanding again but this time he took a step too far. Hitler had always hated the Slavic races. He thought them to be a lazy and pretty useless people. He decided to move against his ally Stalin, thinking that his armies would succeed in destroying the Russian armies in a relatively short space of time. However, Hitler had not allowed for the vast expanses of Russia and the winter weather which raged across the country. This miscalculation was probably Hitler's greatest mistake and the key reason for him in ultimately losing the war. The Russians deliberately retreated and continued to absorb Hitler's pursuing armies towards Moscow. The Germans were simply not prepared logistically to make such a long march. Many Germans died in that frightful and bleak winter. The damages to Hitler's armies were considerable.

The Russians, having now joined the Allied Forces against Germany, released the Polish prisoners-of-war and told them to go and fight the Germans wherever they could find them. A momentous irony.

On 26th April 1943 there were 500,000 Polish soldiers imprisoned in the Soviet Union. There were about 150 concentration camps designated for the Polish army, among those were 99 built in Soviet-occupied areas of Poland. They housed about 100,000 officers and soldiers.

The Polish officers grasped this new opportunity with considerable enthusiasm even though they were being released in terrible physical condition. Poles living there had one aim – to fight for the freedom of Poland. In the space of a few weeks over 40,000 men, from different parts of the Soviet Union, assembled in a newly formed Polish army.

Tadeusz and his friends managed to secure a lorry and they agreed to set out on a daunting journey across the spine of Russia down towards Persia (now Iran). They obtained some small food stocks but not nearly enough for their ambitious journey. The lorry carried around 40 soldiers. Every two or three days, they had to remove fellow soldiers who had died overnight, of malnutrition. When they eventually arrived, only half of the soldiers taking the original journey had survived. They had achieved their first planned destination in Tockoye, a city in eastern Siberia en route to their final destination in Persia. Tadeusz was immediately hospitalised as he was suffering badly from malaria. It took him two months to recover. Life was still a slender thread, but he had survived.

CHAPTER 3

It was here in Tockoye, that Tadeusz first met
Maria. His horrendous experiences in the previous
four years had long ago wiped away any thoughts of
finding Ella, his fiancée, or even knowing if she was
still alive. The war had destroyed Europe. There were
no communications back to Poland. His life had
moved on in so many different ways.

When he met Maria, it was more to party with
fellow soldiers to celebrate survival. The Poles loved
their vodka and they were able to deal with copious
amounts from the Russians in Tockoye. Tadeusz,
now fully recovered from malaria, partied with his
friends almost every night. Life was considered short
and fun was considered mandatory before they had to

go back into the frays of war. Tadeusz spent a lot of his time with his new friend Maria. They spoke about their journeys to Tockoye and how they had spent their previous four years in these wretched times. Neither touched on their previous lives in Poland as it did not seem relevant at the time. Tadeusz felt that he should tell Maria about Ella but decided against it. Another time. Within a few weeks of living in the makeshift army camp Tadeusz was falling in love with this beautiful young girl, who was still then only 20 years of age. Life was cheap in those days. Nobody could rely on any kind of survival. So, to have fallen in love was a blessing. It provided happiness which was not available to anybody. Maria was too in love with this handsome officer. She had never experienced such feelings and she was giddy with his affections.

But soon, various divisions of the Polish armed forces were mobilised, so Tadeusz lost trace of Maria's whereabouts and had to continue on his journey as directed by his army commanders. Eventually, some six months later, the divisions finally arrived in Teheran in Persia. All the Polish forces had gathered in the area.

To his amazement, Tadeusz found Maria again. They met again in an army club that had been thrown together. He was captivated, feeling that he had fallen in love. The war did not hold out much hope for anybody. People lived in the moment and only the moment. The future was a distant entity. The past was irrelevant. Only the now mattered. So, Tadeusz pursued Maria at every opportunity. They spent every moment together, gradually declaring their love to each other and, in a very short time, they decided to get married. People did that during the war as many believed they wouldn't survive. Marriage was an exciting option.

They eventually got married in May 1944. Tadeusz organised some leave to spend time with Maria. They were such happy lovers. Their relationship was new, and they talked about how they would build an exciting life together. They could not begin to consider where they would live as nobody knew where they would be at the end of the war. In truth not many believed that they would still be there at the end. The few days that they managed to enjoy together were beautiful in every way. Two months later Maria realised that she was pregnant, and, at 22 years of age, went to the nearest neutral country, Palestine, where all Polish pregnant mothers went to have their babies. In the summer of 1945, Maria gave birth to their only son, Maciek. They had not planned for a child that soon but were both thrilled to have their new baby boy.

At the end of the war, Poles had few ideas on their next moves. Emigrate to where? Going back to Poland was not possible as it had now been handed over to the Communist regime led by Stalin, who was about to control the entire East European bloc.

Many Poles arrived in Britain at a relatively perilous time. The bravery of Polish pilots and sailors became known in Britain from the first battles with the Germans. Britain needed them and welcomed their arrivals. So it was that Tadeusz, with his young wife Maria and their baby two-year-old son, arrived in Southampton to start a new life.

CHAPTER 4

Maria was one of four sisters. Her parents were Kazimierz and Krasnaroda who owned a huge estate just outside of Poznan. Kazimierz was a local senior judge, so their life was one of luxury and wealth. When the war broke out, Maria's parents were taken as prisoners. Kazimierz, her father, was sent to Dachau concentration camp, where he died two years later.

Maria's sister Halszka, was being taken away to join a mobilisation of Polish forces area in Kazakhstan, Siberia. Maria was still young and didn't want to be left alone in Poznan while the war was raging. So, she volunteered to go with Halszka. At 16 years of age it was a bleak prospect but somehow Maria survived. She had an infectious personality.

Everybody liked this young girl who carried her pride and a smile that enchanted most.

Halszka was engaged to Czechu who was a Colonel in the Polish Army. So, they used their influence and managed to get Maria into the Polish Army, to help with driving soldiers to their various destinations. Maria had learnt to drive on their family estate at a young age when her father had let her drive the cars they owned on their land. So, Maria was now part of the Polish Army at 18 years of age. Her work was almost entirely to do with driving large lorries, full of soldiers, and her first orders took her to Tockoye in Siberia where she first met Tadeusz. They were both immediately smitten with each other, but army movements separated them after a few weeks. As the war continued the Polish soldiers were mobilised to Persia. Eventually in Teheran, Maria bumped into Tadeusz again, as the Polish forces were mostly concentrated in that area. This time they were able to spend time together. So, their love continued to blossom, and eventually they were married in May 1944.

The war ended less than a year later. Tadeusz and

Maria, with their only son, arrived in Southampton. The creation of a Polish community in Great Britain resulted from wartime experiences which few people in the West could have imagined – occupation by both Nazis and Soviets; genocide, deportations, ethnic cleansing, slave labour, the exotic odysseys of homeless and stateless refugees. It was, above all, a moral triumph, a victory of faith and determination over adversities of an extreme kind.

CHAPTER 5

Now, a full 37 years later, Ella appeared back in his life. Through this lone, single letter that had arrived that morning. But only if he allowed her in. Tadeusz tried to examine his feelings. What did he really think about Ella? All he could remember was a 23-year-old beauty who had passed her law degree with honours. And her beautiful smile when she laughed – and she did laugh so much. Tadeusz slowly unravelled his mind back to Warsaw just before the war. He looked at his life then where he lived with his family in a beautiful 200-year-old mansion in Warsaw situated on the banks of the Vistula River coursing through the central city. Life was indeed good then. He had not allowed himself to look back before now.

He did not see the point as he knew it could so easily lead to self-pity and bitterness. He remembered their wedding plans and the 200-odd guests who were due to join them on the first day of his new life with Ella. It felt strange to go back. Like another life. The war had really done its damage and virtually rubbed away his previous life or any memory of it.

He read the letter a third time and tried to imagine Ella writing to him. She had so much passion in her words and it really moved Tadeusz. He was slowly transported back in his mind. Yes, he had been so deeply in love. So young and naïve. It was a beautiful time in his life before the pain and death that he had experienced in the war. He closed his eyes and started to glide back very slowly.

'Tadeusz,' Maria said, shaking him gently. 'How are you feeling? Are you a little better now? You've been asleep for three hours. It's 4pm. Better you stop sleeping so it doesn't affect your night later…'

Tadeusz opened his eyes. He thought he had closed them briefly but had in fact drifted off to his previous existence and that memory, with a calm spirit he felt, had enabled him to sleep. He sat up, slowly stretching and then he spotted the letter under his pillow, the edge slightly protruding. Maria was returning with a cup of black coffee which they often enjoyed in the afternoon. With their cigarettes again.

Tadeusz shifted his weight to conceal the letter. It was way too early in his mind to share it with Maria. He hadn't properly considered the ramifications himself, let alone share them with Maria.

He was sure that he had mentioned his engagement to Maria when they were enjoying an evening in a night club in Teheran. The music in the club had slowed down, as it was 3am. Tadeusz had felt that it was correct to tell Maria. It seemed the right thing to do... perhaps because he had by now fallen in love with her. They returned to their table, poured another vodka for each of them and he started softly to tell Maria of his past commitment before the war. He described how he had met Ella at university and how they had fallen in love. He recounted how they had planned the wedding and then how the war had come and ripped his life to pieces. Maria had held his hand during this conversation, listening attentively. She had never been in love before, although she knew she was in love with Tadeusz. Deeply in love. But Maria was 16 when the war had started so the opportunities to fall in love had not been there. The odd light fling recently with an officer in the army but that's all.

Maria didn't seem too concerned at the time and didn't display any jealous observations. She understood the war and the consequences. But now? Tadeusz suspected that now Maria would want to protect her marriage and would not be happy to learn about the letter. Tadeusz decided to keep it to himself for now.

Days went by, and Tadeusz found himself slowly sinking back into his days in Warsaw. The joy and the love he shared at the time with his young bride-to-be. It was all so wonderful and so happy. Ella had written and she sounded like she was just that same person back then. Her whole heart had been poured into the letter she had sent him. Ella had not restrained herself at all. She had written to the man she once loved, and really had loved so deeply for the whole of her life.

After five days of wandering around in a slight daze it finally came to Tadeusz that he must write back. He wanted to write back. His feelings were that he wanted to express some emotion and not simply reject the first contact from Ella. Maria had been following him around showing genuine concern as she couldn't get under the skin of what was wrong. She instinctively knew it was not his illness or his blood pressure. Something was bothering him, but she could not define the issues that seemed to revolve around their conversations. Certainly, he was being evasive – she knew that.

On Saturday morning, Tadeusz got up with a spring in his step. He knew he had to write. He came in for breakfast, and Maria was immediately relieved to see that the cloud had seemingly lifted from above his head. Tadeusz was back to his old self. In fact, he was better than that. Unusually energetic, Maria thought.

Tadeusz suddenly said: 'I need to go the library to—'

'Library?' she interrupted. 'What will you be doing in the library??'

Tadeusz stretched up to his full frame and said: 'I want to research some history as am writing a piece about Poland before the war… for the Army Society.'

Maria smiled at him. 'That sounds like fun for you,

but could you go tomorrow as it's changeover day today?'

Tadeusz replied: 'It's not open tomorrow and I won't be long – promise!' he said with enthusiasm.

So, they agreed. He would go in the afternoon when most of the essential jobs around the hotel had been completed.

*

Tadeusz walked to the library. Faster than he normally walked, to his surprise. The truth was that he had already started to compose his response. The magic of her letter had touched him deeper than he was prepared to admit. His senses were full of guilt and remorse as he didn't want to keep this from Maria. But somehow the privacy of this first exchange would be better if left intact between him and Ella. And there need not be more than one letter response. Just this one would do it.

Tadeusz was now getting excited. His initial fears and doubts had mostly been swept away with each step from the hotel towards the library. On the way he bumped into Janet Goddard. Janet was a local woman who often popped into the hotel. She was a widow and had a small crush on Tadeusz. Janet thought that she managed to keep that secret to herself. But Maria had spotted it long ago and occasionally teased Tadeusz about it.

'Good morning, Janet!' Tadeusz offered with the smile of a man who was on a mission.

Janet jumped. 'Oh, good morning Tadeusz… Why are you so chirpy this morning?' she asked, eyes twinkling at him. Tadeusz was not usually so forthcoming, so it took her unawares. But she was pretty enthusiastic about this chance meeting, without Maria always appearing whenever Janet did visit them.

'Oh, nothing much,' replied Tadeusz, turning for a second. 'I'm just popping to the library. To get a book,' he added as if to ensure that his plan to write to Ella remained a firm secret for now. And off he went down the hill at a decent pace. Janet hurried off, slightly perplexed, in the other direction.

Tadeusz arrived at the library. He had plain paper in his backpack which he had taken earlier from the hotel. So, he settled in at the first available desk and took a deep breath. Eventually he let it out and sighed. His first thought was to go back to 1939 when he was a young graduate ready to marry his beloved Ella. He closed his eyes and allowed himself to drift. It was not easy as he had long ago removed that whole life from his mind. The horrors of war had caused him to move on and to forget. Tadeusz had never thought back, especially after he had met and married Maria. That life was long gone. Until now.

Tadeusz was faced with a huge dilemma. His memories of Ella had grown hour by hour in his mind. He remembered so much more about their time together back before the war. He wanted to say so much. To match her passion with his own words, his own emotions. But he could not deny his love for Maria. Even in secret he could not gush to Ella. He could not open his heart in the same way. Not now. And not yet.

He decided to read Ella's emotional letter again. Certainly, that helped as he was no longer panicking. Maria nowhere to be seen. He could absorb the whole of the letter and all its implications. He had made up his mind to write back with honesty and integrity. Neither of those words promised too much.

My dearest Ella,

As you can imagine I was deeply shocked and so excited to get your letter. Just so completely amazed that you are alive and more, that you have found me. I received it yesterday and have been reeling from the passion in the words which you expressed to me.

I confess that my hand is shaking while writing this letter back to you. An extraordinary surprise and a wonderful moment in my life to be able to speak to you again. I am really not sure where to start. So much to say that I am lost for words.

Most importantly I want to thank you from the very pit of my soul for finding me. And for writing those beautiful words to me. I did hear about the desperately sad loss of my parents from other family members. And I was decimated by the news about Henryk being taken to Auschwitz and perishing there only 10 months later. How are your parents? What happened to you in Warszawa after the final destruction of the city? I need to ask so much as my knowledge of that time is very limited. Not many people survived to tell the stories or bring back the news.

But more importantly you. And me. How my life changed in so many ways since I last saw you at that restaurant – that picture has always stayed with me in my heart. I was taken that night to a Siberian concentration camp where I knew I would die. Most inmates died within 12 months of arrival, so I didn't hold out much hope. During those early months, I could not think of anything else but us. Our life at University. Our plans for the wedding. The life we had created. The house we had decided to buy by the river. It was all going to be so magical. And most of all I cherished the love that we had shared.

But now in that camp, I knew we were a dream of the past. I could see the other older inmates. Thin with malnutrition. Only weeks to survive. And I believed that my turn was soon coming. So, I stopped hoping. I stopped thinking about us. I couldn't bear the pain. My emotions were raw. Your beauty was overwhelming, consuming my mind. So, I actively began to drift away from you and from the past. I could no longer think about what might have been...

Then suddenly the Russians announced a change. They had decided to join the Allies. Rumours were that the Germans had turned to attack the Russian Empire and had failed. So now the Allies were looking for every person who could help destroy the German advances. For me, and for my friends, there was no choice. We were given a lorry with fuel supplies and told to find the Allied Forces in Persia to fight the Germans. We were free.

Ella, I was a broken man. No longer did I carry memories.

Just an instinct for survival. When we finally arrived in Teheran some four weeks later, only half of my friends survived with me. I was suffering from acute malaria. God knows how I got that, but our immune systems were empty. We had nothing left. So, you can imagine how my mind was no longer connected to anything to do with our time before the war. It was a distant past. Please forgive me if that sounds weak on my part, but we had been walking with death for well over a year.

And I now come to the most difficult part of my letter, Ella, my darling.

In Teheran we all believed that our days were numbered. Unlikely that we would survive the war. We were all so strongly motivated to join the Allied Forces and to go after those Germans who had destroyed our beloved country. The Germans who destroyed you and me?

Our focus was to survive enough to help deal any kind of blow to the Germans. Nothing else mattered. We partied for a few weeks in Tehran before we were to be advanced to Monte Cassino in Italy. Our parties were heavy with vodka and we all indulged in our last days on earth. Then I met Maria. We fell in love and very soon after we got married. All the time having grave doubts about the possibility of survival. Maria became pregnant and was shipped to Palestine with other Polish pregnant mothers and I returned to Monte Cassino to see out the last remnants of the war. The Germans were throwing everything they could at us as we knew their time was coming to an end. Now I had to survive. I had a wife and son. I could not lose them as well, after losing you.

Ella, I cannot apologise for them being part of my life as I love them both so very much. As I am sure that you love your husband and five sons. Having got this far with my letter, I realise that I am feeling guilty for not finding you after the war. It was impossible for us to return with Stalin's control of Poland. And I had given up on the past. And on our love.

But now I am so thrilled to hear from you. I am so excited but don't really know how to express my deeper feelings? To know that you are alive and well. And you have become a Judge?? How is that even possible? In my mind you are still a beautiful young and innocent girl who had just passed the bar. You laughed and giggled frequently, taking very little too seriously. Well I must congratulate you! Not because you achieved this exalted position, but because it is so distant from where I last saw you a few weeks before our wedding. My dearest Ella, I am so proud that you achieved the highest legal status in our beloved Poland.

For my part, my law degree offered me no positions in

England. I couldn't speak English. So, I started work in a restaurant washing dishes. It brought in the food and provided us with somewhere to live. But we were happy that we had survived and could build a new life in a country that readily adopted us after serving our part the war. And over the years, I got more and more involved in catering leading me to buy the restaurant where I had started as a dishwasher. I enjoyed that enormously. Eventually when my son, Maciek, had reached 20 years of age, Maria and I decided to move to Bournemouth by the sea to semi-retire and where we bought a small hotel. And that's where you have found me 37 years after I left you in Warszawa. Probably the worst day of my life.

My darling Ella, I hope that some of these words have served to explain why I abandoned you in Warszawa. It was truly hopeless to find a way back. And so, life moved on. Every day just survival. And now you have found me again and written such beautiful words to me. I felt your passion which burned right into my soul. You were my first true love. And now 37 years have passed, and you are a Judge almost ready for retirement. And I am semi-retired in the UK.

I am not sure that I can say more at this stage as my whole being is turned upside down. I am glad that I have been able to write to you freely and to tell you more about me and my life.

But can I tell you how I feel deep inside? I am not sure that I know myself yet. So, I need to end this letter on that note. If you choose to reply, then I will very gladly read your thoughts whatever they might be.

My darling Ella. Thank you for finding me and thank you from the bottom of my heart for writing. We have experienced a lifetime apart so now would be good to discover us again.

Your Tadeusz

Tadeusz stood up and stretched. He had been fixed in his position while carefully penning his words to Ella. He hoped he had been positive in his response and enthusiastic to help her reply soon... He would have liked to have been more emotive but, in his heart, he knew it was too soon. Too easy to just spill open and then what? How did he deal with that and his feelings for Maria? On the one hand his excitement was mounting, and he knew it would get worse. On the other hand, he had to remind himself that only two days ago his life was quiet, calm and without any stresses. Mostly thanks to Maria.

He walked briskly to the Post Office. He wanted to send the letter before he rewrote or, even worse, changed his mind about sending any kind of reply. It didn't take long. The Post Office was only a five-minute walk away. He got there, sealed the letter in the envelope and posted with the required stamps.

A huge relief swept over him. He had done the right thing. After all, Ella had been his first love. She deserved to hear from him. But now the wait. Tadeusz was astounded how quickly he wanted a reply. The letter had not even been collected from the Post Office and already he was calculating how long it would take to get to Ella. And how long for her to respond. He calmed himself and started the journey back to the hotel, and to Maria.

He got back only three hours after leaving. Maria was finishing the Saturday swap day chores. She was glad to be rid of Tadeusz as he only got under her feet. Asking inane questions about the bookings, which she had covered many times. So, as she was just getting into her usual afternoon, Tadeusz swept in slightly flushed.

'Hi, my darling!' he exclaimed a little too enthusiastically. Maria looked at him and wondered what had gotten into him. He was not prone to sweep in, nor to be so exuberant.

'I'm fine. And how was your library trip? Do you want a coffee?' she asked.

'Yes please,' he replied. 'Library was predictably dull. And very quiet. I did my research and made some notes, so I really enjoyed my time. Thanks.' He wanted to close the conversation as he didn't want to continue with the lie. He knew one day he would have to tell Maria about Ella's letter. He dreaded that day.

Maria knew her man. She detected that he was closing down on her. But their subject was not interesting enough to make her want to explore his reluctance to talk. She had too much to do.

CHAPTER 6

Ella had sent her letter. Not much hope of a reply, but she nurtured a burning desire to hear from her Tadeusz. Would he get the letter? Yes, of course he would; she knew his address from a good friend in the UK. So how long would it take for him to reply? Maybe he wouldn't reply? The questions raced around in her mind, day after day. She could not focus on anything much. Her whole existence had changed since she discovered that her Tadeusz was still alive and well. Ella had cleanly divided her normal life with her work, her husband Witold and their five sons, and her new determination to find Tadeusz.

Now nearly two weeks had passed since she posted the letter. It seemed an eternity. Day after day, meaningless letters dropped through their front door. It was seriously frustrating and increasingly upsetting. But Ella held on in the belief that Tadeusz would write. He must write. She still believed she knew him. Or was that a ridiculous notion? Not much made sense. Logic was now irrelevant.

Then it arrived. With a stamp from England. It hit the floor like a thunderclap. Ella grabbed it and swept it into her pocket. She had been at the door every morning waiting for her postman. Ella felt like a teenager. Certainly, she didn't resemble a respected senior judge in Poland. She laughed at her behaviour. Ridiculous. How was this possible? But she knew that it was real and possible. She did feel like a teenager. The same girl she was when she first met her love, Tadeusz.

Ella jumped in her car. Went straight to her office in the city and locked the door behind her. She could not and would not be interrupted. Not now.

She opened the letter slowly. Tried to be calm and be prepared to be let down. But her Tadeusz had replied so her joy was complete.

Slowly Ella read the letter. Tears poured from her

eyes. She recognised his words and the way he spoke. Even after all these years, she knew this was her Tadeusz writing to her. He was wonderful with his words of affection. Yet he was practical and not over emotive. He kept a balance. But she knew that he was thrilled to hear from her – she understood it between the lines and not in the words themselves. Ella re-read the letter five times before she was able to put it down. Now she had committed it to memory; she could almost recite every thought if not every word. *My Tadeusz is alive and is talking to me again,* she thought. After 30 years of wilderness. Ella felt whole again. That day back then, when her Tadeusz was ripped from her life, had never left her. No matter what she did with her life, Tadeusz had always been with her inside her heart.

In the next 20 minutes, various people would expect Ella to act as a senior judge, so she had to remove herself from being 19 again. She had to come back to the now. The present. Life had to go on. Ella had a serious function in life and a family to care for. Perhaps an ordeal but one that she grasped, as always, with responsibility. She continued her next days, mostly relying on her considerable skills to deal with legal matters, all the time thinking of the words that her Tadeusz had sent to her.

The weekend eventually arrived, and Ella with husband and two of her younger sons, prepared to go to their lodge in the mountains which they frequently visited as a family. It was a beautiful retreat. Both Ella and Witold often took their legal papers and would finish off their week's work while the boys went off climbing in the Tatra mountains.

On the first evening there, Ella was working quietly by the fireplace. She often sat there with her case files. Witold had gone to bed earlier as he was tired from the week's stresses in court. He needed to rest.

Ella decided to read the letter again. She could use this opportunity to reply as well. A burning desire to write back to Tadeusz had been with her for most of the week. She decided that the time was right. She needed to get her thoughts on paper to him.

My dearest Tadeusz,

You cannot possibly imagine how excited I was to receive your reply. Somehow just that one letter from you has made me complete. I now realise that I have existed with a piece of me, of my heart, missing. Never to be repaired. And now you have put me back together. My soul sings and my heart feel at peace.

I am sitting here in my mountain lodge. My husband Witold and two of my boys are asleep. The fire is blazing. And you are sitting opposite me as a ghost-like figure. With your wonderful smile and looking so young and handsome! Just as I have always remembered you, day by day, during these past 30 years.

Of course, I know that you must have changed, as I have too. Goodness we have both lived a life of so many years since we last were together. But for now, you are sitting opposite me in the glowing fire, and that is all I need. I feel so close to you again. I have read your wonderful letter and understand why you must also consider your feelings about Maria.

I am just so happy that you are really alive and it's no longer a distant rumour. That my Tadeusz did survive and now has spoken to me. It is beyond all that I hoped and cherished during the early years, after our separation. Eventually, after the first few years, I had to put you to the back of my mind, but I always lived with some deep instinct that you had not yet left this world. Or me.

I am looking at you, glimmering in the light, as you watch me writing back to you. I'm still in a dreamy state just smiling inside that I have you back in my life. Even though there is such a distance between us.

I am glad that you are so happy and that you found a new life with your Maria and Maciek. Would it be wrong to ask about them? How are you as a husband and father? How have you enjoyed your years in England building your home for your family? I have so many questions to ask you… If I am honest, these questions are really about how I imagine our lives would have been had we been allowed to build our lives together. Before I met Witold, I often imagined us having children. Making a home. Spending time together in the mountains that we both loved so much. But eventually I had to move on for my own sanity. It was not healthy living a life with you as my fictional partner.

So, you can see why I am just so deliriously happy that you are indeed alive and that I have had your reply to complete our contact.

I do not harbour any regrets as I love my five boys and, perhaps I would not have had them had we stayed together by some miracle? So, we cannot regret the way life has developed for us individually and collectively.

Tadeusz you sit there smiling at me while I write. I can almost touch your beautiful face. It's extraordinary for me to have such a strong image of you, in front of me. This moment, by the fire, I will never forget. The feelings that are churning inside of me as I speak to you.

I am now having to consider the realities of both of our worlds. I am curious whether you told Maria of my letter to you? Did you let her read it? Or did you keep it to yourself for now? I am dreading telling Witold. I did consider telling him that I had discovered your address from a distant friend. But I was sure that I could not yet tell him how deeply I felt and all that I have been able to say to you in my letters.

Deep in my heart I so hope that we could continue to talk to each other forever. I know, I know it's maybe crazy to have thoughts like that… But it's how I feel. I am still beyond words about the fact that you are in my life again. Even if only so minimally.

Darling Tadeusz, please tell me about you and how you feel today? I need to understand your truthful thoughts. Your feelings about my letters. But is my passion too much for you? I so hope that what I say to you brings back your feelings for our lost love… Please write soon Tadeusz as I am lost without your words. The fire is now dying, and the embers just hold your glow. But you are slowly disappearing as the light drops away in my room. Goodnight, my darling. I will wait for your reply… sending you all my love and huge embraces close to your heart.

Ella

CHAPTER 7

Tadeusz, having sent his letter, was now reaching a state of mild anxiety. For the first time in his life he felt that, in some way, he was cheating on his Maria. He knew that to hold a secret of this magnitude was not fair on Maria, yet he wanted it to be his private knowledge only for the foreseeable future. He considered his options and all of them led back to not saying anything for now. He justified it thinking that after a couple of letter exchanges the communication with Ella would subside and drift away. The problem with that thinking was that Tadeusz knew in his heart that this was not going to be a quick exchange. He knew from the passion she had expressed that she wanted to know him in almost the way he was back then when they were young lovers to be married. So, he decided that he would wait to see Ella's reply.

The week went by slowly. Tadeusz spent most of his day in his tool shed. He loved his tools. He was not too good at DIY but he did like to pretend that he was busy keeping the hotel in good shape. Every few months he would call Arek, a local Polish builder, to pop by and make sure that all the plumbing and fixings were in good order. The work gave him a feeling of personal satisfaction as each day he drifted around the grounds in his overalls. But mainly this role that he had given himself, meant that he did not need to speak to hotel guests or get involved in their daily needs. Maria was so good at that. She could talk to the guests all day long. In fact, she could out-talk them so that, as the week went by, they bothered her less and less. Mission accomplished.

Tadeusz often spent his evenings serving in the hotel bar. He liked that job as he could expound on his political theories with the guests. He would indulge himself with a couple of glasses of red wine through the course of the evening. The guests liked the bar, so it was rewarding for Tadeusz to consider this, his own personal contribution to the success of their little hotel.

That particular evening, his great friend Stefan was there, sharing a drink, as a guest. They had known each other for many years right back to the time when they came to England after the war. Tadeusz felt he could share private things with Stefan and rely on his discretion. So, he toyed with talking to Stefan about Ella… He was wondering whether that would be a step too far when Stefan asked him: 'A penny for your thoughts, Tadeusz? You are unusually quiet tonight…'

'Mm. I know. I've been wrestling with some personal issues,' Tadeusz replied. 'Just too much going on right now,' he added with a slight murmur.

Stefan looked from his drink with a puzzled face, as he knew Tadeusz well. And he knew that it was unusual for Tadeusz to even mention his private thoughts.

'You want to share anything with me, Tadeusz?' he asked.

Tadeusz looked at Stefan for a long while without speaking. Suddenly he decided to tell Stefan everything. About the letters. So, he did. He slowly outlined the whole story from the start. Stefan was seriously attentive. He never moved or even tried to respond. He was in a slight state of shock. He had known Tadeusz and Maria right back in 1947 when they had all arrived in England. They had shared many a lively party with considerable amounts of vodka. They all had spent good times together after the war.

Now Tadeusz was telling him a story which was beyond shock. And as Tadeusz explained the developments, Stefan also knew that his friend was already becoming deeply committed to Ella and involved in a deception with Maria. Tadeusz omitted the depth of feelings expressed by him and Ella in the letters. But even the superficial descriptions moved Stefan. He had experienced his own losses back in Poland, so he understood Tadeusz. But these letters were really deeply emotional. In Stefan's opinion, they were very difficult for Tadeusz to deal with.

After some 20 minutes of words streaming from Tadeusz, Stefan held up his hand and said: 'Tadeusz, do you have any idea at all, where you are taking this? What do you honestly think will happen next, my friend?'

Tadeusz stopped talking. He pondered and opened his hands with a sigh. 'I really don't know, Stefan. It has knocked me sideways. I just don't know, nor do I understand where I am with it all.' Tadeusz looked down at the bar, not really sure what he was going to say next.

After a while, he looked up at Stefan. He shook his head and said: 'I think I've gone a little too far with it. OK, there have only been two letters, but so full of emotion. Of declared love. All the old feelings flooding back. My thoughts keep racing around in my head with no conclusions at all!' he spluttered.

Stefan stepped around the bar and embraced his old friend. Tadeusz, not used to signs of affection from any of his friends, gratefully accepted the hug. He needed one.

Stefan stepped back to the customer side of the small bar and asked for another glass of red wine. He then added: 'Have you thought about when you might share the broad story with Maria? You cannot really keep it a secret for much longer. For your own sake as well as Maria's.'

'I know,' replied Tadeusz. 'I thought initially that I

would tell Maria, but Ella's flow of words has captured me so much that I'm not sure how much I can possibly tell her. Maria is such a strong person and I think would understand, but she will also see straight through me. And will know how confused I am about the whole saga.'

'But what do you really think you feel, Tadeusz?' asked Stefan. 'That has to be your next honest question to yourself.'

Tadeusz pondered the question. He nodded slowly. 'God, I know you're so right. And I do know that I have to tell her soon. But I need more time. Stefan, you know full well that Ella was my first love. She deserves my answers and time from me without worrying about Maria or her husband Witold's involvement. That has to be the right thing to do… What do you think?'

Stefan knew that it was futile to dissuade Tadeusz. Had been on the receiving end of his resolve before. Tadeusz had made up his mind and was not going to be moved.

'OK. I do understand. It had to be a huge shock for you, and I appreciate the need to get some kind of closure with Ella. But you know how much I care for you and Maria. You are my best friends. It would be tragic to destroy or even affect what you have both built here.'

Stefan looked directly at Tadeusz. 'Be very careful with your next steps, my dear friend. It's very important that you go carefully and hold on to your strong sense of logic. It's always looked after you in the past, and you will need it more now than ever before.'

With that, Stefan finished his glass. Set it down and kissed Tadeusz on both cheeks. He bade him goodnight and left to go to his room.

Tadeusz stood there alone in the bar. The guests had gone to bed. He was left with his own deep thoughts before retiring himself to the bedroom. Maria was already asleep and curled up in her usual foetal position. Tadeusz stripped, and eased himself into bed. He lay on his back and started thinking. Drifting. Eyes closing. Back to Warszawa and his time there before the war.

The next morning seemed to be the same as usual. But Maria could see him fidgeting. Sometimes staring vaguely into the distance. He had to camouflage his deepest thoughts. His mind was almost entirely focused in anticipation of Ella's reply.

And so, the days passed, each almost identical to the next. Maria struck up small conversations about the hotel issues, and Tadeusz was able to reply constructively to the small problems. But Maria knew he was not entirely there. She knew him better than he knew himself. Maria kept her peace. She believed that these things eventually find a way to the top. The story would unfold. She was just hoping that it was not something serious... Perhaps he was seriously ill? Or did he have some other financial problem with his taxes? But never, with all her honed instincts, could Maria know the real core of what was troubling her Tadeusz. *Time will tell,* she thought, but she would eventually have to ask him to help her understand. Whatever it was that troubled him.

Then on Thursday, some 15 days after he had sent his letter, the postman ambled down the long path to the hotel. Tadeusz was just sorting a heating problem in one of the guest rooms, and Maria was explaining, to a guest, the route to the gardens in the main square. The postman reached the front door and saw

Maria just inside.

'Hi Maria,' he exclaimed. 'Haven't seen you for a while... Where is Tadeusz? Is he not feeling well?'

Maria stepped forward. 'Hi, Frank. Yes, nice to see you again. It's been too long. Tadeusz is dealing with... Oh. Here he is now!' Tadeusz was already hurrying forward to grab the post. But too late. Maria had already taken a firm grip on the letters. She swung round to give them to Tadeusz, but suddenly stopped.

'What's the hurry?' she said, puzzled by his apparent enthusiasm to get the letters.

'Oh no, nothing at all,' he said. 'I am waiting for a letter from the Council about our rates,' he mumbled. He hated himself for this new lie.

Maria was not convinced but shrugged her shoulders and gave him the letters. She hurried off to deal with more guests who were leaving for the beach and wanted a packed lunch.

Tadeusz looked at the letters he was holding, or even squeezing. He knew straight away that the second letter peeping through had a Polish stamp. *Oh, my goodness,* he thought. *Ella has replied.* At last.

Tadeusz rocked on his heels. Breathless with a

mixture of guilt and excitement, he scurried off back to his desk. He always had peace there as Maria was only too happy to leave him with his papers. It meant that she could get on and also find a little quiet time to herself. Reading detective novels was Maria's favourite pastime. And a couple of hours per day were her best moments.

Tadeusz sat down with a thump. At last. He would soon know how to deal with this whole bizarre episode. He tore open the letter. He hurried through the first few paragraphs but then slowed. He needed to absorb the words, not hurry past them. He started at the beginning again and slowly read each word. Each sentence.

He put the letter down and let out a long sigh. He was so enthralled by her words. He smiled to himself at her descriptions of her time writing by the fireplace. He remembered how they had discussed their desires to own a small lodge in the mountains. And now Ella had written to him from her own lodge. How poignant, he thought. He picked up the letter and slowly digested the words all over again. He loved the purity of her words. Written from the heart.

Written without conditions. Just Ella as she was back then, some 30 years ago. Tadeusz was overcome with the joy that he experienced when reading the words. He put the letter away in his jacket pocket and leaned back in his chair with eyes closed. He smiled to himself. He had forgotten how it was to be deeply in love, immersed in all that passion. Yes, he knew how much he loved Maria, but this new emotion flooded his being. He had never imagined that, in the autumn of his life, that he would feel like this again.

CHAPTER 8

At that moment Maria brought in his coffee, as he had been at his desk too long. He jumped with a jolt, opening his eyes to focus on Maria walking towards him, cup in hand.

'Oh, hi,' he exclaimed rather clumsily. Maria nodded back, thinking that this man was not her Tadeusz. He was behaving oddly but certainly he wasn't ill, she surmised.

'Here's your coffee.' Maria sat on the bed near his desk and sipped her own coffee while watching him intently. What was bothering her man?

'I am just thinking about the extension we've been thinking about building,' he said weakly. Maria's immediate conclusion was that his problem did not seem to be a financial burden of any description, if he was talking of spending money on an extension.

'Oh. And what were you thinking? Did you get the planning permission back yet from the Council?' she asked.

'Well, it occurred to me that we could start laying the foundations, as our architect told me that there would not be any problem with planning. We just have to wait for the final formalities.' Tadeusz stood up to flex his limbs and fidgeted with his papers on the desk. Desperately buying time to get himself back to normal life with Maria. He couldn't possibly reveal the secret that was burning a hole in his jacket pocket!

'I think that it would be good if you could start thinking about the materials needed for the interiors of the three rooms.' Tadeusz thought that this diversion was an excellent tactic as he knew Maria loved to be creative with interior designing and would relish the opportunity to break the daily routine that was her life in the hotel.

Of course, Maria spotted the diversion almost before the words had left his mouth. She had anticipated that he would try to change the subject.

And now he was giving her the chance to start the creative process of buying what would be needed. Fine, she thought. Maria decided to go with the new plans, while thinking about when she might eventually have to challenge him about his anxiety. They had reached an invisible stalemate, both needing to go about the business of running a hotel. They finished their coffees in an awkward silence and went back to the main hall where most things happened during the day.

Four whole days went by and Tadeusz simply couldn't find a moment to write a reply to Ella, the woman he once loved with all of his soul. He had grabbed a few opportunities to re-read the letter and absorb the beautiful words written to him. But he just couldn't reply. Not yet anyway.

Finally, on Monday, he found an excuse to go and visit his accountant on the other side of Bournemouth. He told Maria that he would be going the next morning and would be gone for a few hours, but back in time for lunch. Maria had her doubts about the accountant visit but again chose to let it go.

Tadeusz drove off the next morning and wound through the back streets towards the side part of the town. There was some easy parking there, which allowed him to find a nice coffee bar where he could sit and write in peace. At last he started to reconnect with Ella again. He locked the car and walked across the road to the café. He asked for a strong coffee and settled into the comfortable armchair facing a low round table. After a few minutes of initial quietness, he took out the paper and started to write his reply. To his Ella. By now any thoughts of Maria and the hotel he had left behind. His mind was moving back to the mountains where he had spent many years of his childhood climbing and rambling. He was connecting again with Ella in her lodge from where she had written to him.

My darling Ella,

It was so wonderful to hear back from you so soon. I need to tell you that I find your letters to be so beautiful and inspiring. You have brought me back to our time together and shared with me our beloved mountains where we often went for our summer holidays. I remember those times so well now. I have spent a lot of time wondering how it was that I had removed almost all of the past from my thoughts and especially from my memories.

The war had such a powerful way of erasing any thoughts of the past. All that seemed to matter was to survive. And to survive sufficiently to help friends fight the war against the Germans, for stealing our lives. And stealing our country. So, we fought. We did not stop to think about what we had left behind nor what we had lost. We were numb. We could only think of the moment. The now. And that was every day in the camps in Siberia. And then every minute during our ordeal to get back to civilisation and regroup to continue fighting our war.

There was no time to dwell on the pain of loss. No opportunity to reflect on what might have been. And most of all no time for self-pity. We all knew that those thoughts were seriously destructive. We had witnessed good friends indulging in the negativity of the war and all its damage. And these same friends frequently lost their way and ultimately died. They had lost their focus for survival.

In the earlier months and years, I did think hard about my life back then in our beautiful city of Warszawa. How we spent our time together. About my beloved parents who had created such a wonderful life for us all. But the daily horrors soon swept these thoughts aside. I had to find food each day. I was losing weight through starvation and malnutrition. The months went by without hope of being rescued. The challenge was to survive each day.

So, my darling, you can imagine how difficult it was to spare a moment to reflect on the past. And how dangerous it was to the psyche to live looking backwards instead of only going forward.

And now you have brought me back to those times again, that we shared together. I am amazed that I have stored so many memories which have been reborn, often thinking of the smallest details of our days at university. It was such a pure time with the whole world at our feet. So many plans and so much hope for our future. And then I quickly arrive at the moment when it all crashed around us, when I was taken that fateful night. It seems so surreal now.

I loved your letter and the conversation you had with me in your lodge at night-time, next to the fire. It made my heart swell with happiness that you had so much courage to simply tell me how deeply you felt.

But I need to share with you the confusion I am suffering with keeping this a secret from my Maria. I know she does not deserve for me to have this secret, yet I want it to stay with me, at least for now. To enjoy what time, I can with you before I have to tell Maria about our letters. I feel that while it's still a secret, then I am reliving us back then when we were young and so innocent. I must confess that I am so enthralled by your letters and your words of affection. I have also discovered how much I still love you even though we never had the opportunity to live the life that we had planned together.

But I also know that there is no future in this rekindled love. I have no idea where it can take us nor how to contain it within myself while leading the life that I have been used to leading these past 37 years. I have loved my Maria deeply and without limits. She has been wonderful as my partner in the life we have created together with my son in England.

I have never really believed that a person can love two people equally and at the same time. Yet I am living that moment right now, because you found me. And expressed so much love in your letters.

Honestly Ella, I intended to write back to you and express my new rediscovered feelings for you but, I did not mean to share with you, the pain it is causing me. I feel the guilt and am not comfortable with the deceptions. In all these years, I have never veered from the happiness in my life with Maria and Maciek. Yes, we struggled in the earlier years. We had nothing. My law degree was of no value as the law in England is based on an entirely different system. And I could not speak English so that didn't help either. I told you the rest about how I worked in a restaurant and then, eventually, we bought the small hotel. Maria and I really worked very hard to build what we now have here in Bournemouth. So, I know that she deserves not to be treated this way by my maintaining the secret.

How do I share that with her? I am already panicking writing this second letter as that will mean that we will have shared so much together before I share it with Maria – as I know absolutely that I must tell her of our exchanges.

Have you considered telling Witold? And if so, when will you tell him and what details will you share? Because once we tell our partners then I am afraid that it will all become tarnished and the beauty of our thoughts will be stained...

I am sorry to load you with my anxieties. It was not my intention to do that. Not yet anyway.

I was thinking earlier about our times together. Do you remember when I took you out on a punt on the river? When it was such a beautifully hot day. We spent over two hours on the river and eventually moored by that huge willow tree to get some shade. You had prepared that divine picnic with so much delightful food, enough to feed another six people. And I had proposed... What a moment for us both. That day has come back to me and is now imprinted so clearly on my mind. The way your sweet face broke into a huge smile and you shed a *small tear running down your cheek. And you burst into laughter as you hugged me on the grass. We rolled over and over laughing together, and I had to stop us from rolling off the bank and into the water... That was a golden day in my life. In our lives. I had told my parents that I was going to propose, and they were so thrilled, although to be fair they had assumed that there would be a proposal coming soon. And I remember how I had to ask for your hand in marriage from your father. That was a tense moment for me, as he was always such an imposing man. Of course, I had nothing to be concerned about as I knew how fond of me were both your parents. And so, we set the date. Only 8 months later were we to be married. And the friends we would invite... Now I know that so many of them died in that most terrible of wars. I don't have any connections with any of them from those days we shared. Dear Ella, are you in contact with anybody from back then? Have you shared your new knowledge of my survival with any of the friends we shared?*

So, what should we do now? I have little idea except I know how I enjoy writing to you and can imagine doing this for some time to come. Remembering those times, we had together. I would hate for that to be taken away now that you have found me...

I would really enjoy hearing from you again soon. And

please remind me of the days back then. Any anecdotal stories as my memories have been blurred by the war and the travels to England and a new future. Please share with me some stories of then and of now. I want to have a picture of how you are now and what you do in your daily life? Perhaps we should exchange up to date pictures of each other? In my mind you are still 24 years of age and a beautiful young bride of my mine, waiting to be married in the late hot summer in our Warszawa.

For my part I am now old and no longer that person you describe by your fireside. But my soul is the same.

Please write soon. All my love. Tadeusz.

He sat back and paused. Had he gone too far? Had he declared his undying love too much? Had he been disloyal to his Maria? The questions spun around in his head and he knew the answer to all of them was 'yes'.

But that did not deter him from sliding the folded letter into the envelope and sealing it with a determination that would erode his guilt-ridden thoughts. He paid for his three coffees that he had enjoyed during the letter-writing and set off to the Post Office to send the letter before he had time to reflect and change his mind. Tadeusz was now set on a course that he was afraid would control him and his way forward. He knew he was cheating on Maria. That was now clear. He knew that he had finally crossed the line by expressing his deep emotions to the woman he once loved and once had promised to love for all eternity.

Tadeusz arrived at the Post Office and paused. He knew that the letter in his pocket contained words that could not be withdrawn. He understood that, whilst his first letter was enthusiastic, it was also a perfectly reasonable reply. The letter he was about to post was a considerably more open and serious show of affection and even about lost love.

The pause did not last for long. He strode inside, paid for the required stamps, and handed over the letter for overseas post. Done. And now followed the immediate dread of waiting for the reply. In his heart he knew that his behaviour was unreasonable. He knew that there was no future in this new relationship. He understood that it was a personal indulgence in emotions that he had not felt for some time. Experience in life was already warning him to consider the longer-term effects on Ella and Maria. And how he would be responsible for the carnage that would follow. Tadeusz did consider it for a short while, but he was not ready to discard the last six weeks since that first fateful letter had arrived one ordinary spring morning.

CHAPTER 9

Tadeusz walked back to the hotel at a brisk pace. The adrenaline was driving his steps. Soon he arrived back home and went to the kitchen to have a coffee. Maria was already there with a half-finished cup. She looked up to see if she could see any signs of explanation to what was now brewing in her mind as an incongruous situation. What was clear was that Tadeusz had not behaved like this at any stage in their lives as far back as she could remember. Yes, she was sure, that at no stage had he behaved this oddly.

Tadeusz on the other hand, believed that he had it all under control. He had successfully camouflaged his activities from any suspicions expressed by Maria. So, they both skirted around pretending that all was as normal. Maria was slightly shocked that her Tadeusz was so typically male in his actions. Did he not realise that when two people lived with each other 24 hours per day, the slightest shift in behaviour would become immediately visible? It was incredulous to her that he could not see that.

Maria asked: 'Was your visit useful? Did the accountant sort out some good solutions for you?'

Tadeusz gushed with a prepared speech about how they had found the right answers. He complained about the lack of imagination from the accountant, and he explained how he had himself offered some thoughts on ways in which they could reduce the tax exposure. Clever tax evasion, not avoidance. Maria listened to the litany of conversations that they apparently had enjoyed in the accountant's office but not much believing any of it. Maria was now becoming very curious about the underlying truth that seemed to be missing.

Maria did not think that her Tadeusz was having any kind of affair. She thought him to be way too old to bother. She knew that he loved his hotel and his life there with Maria. So, if not an affair, what on earth could be driving this odd behaviour? But above all she knew that he could not sustain it for long before they would find a way to confront the issue. Maria decided to bide her time for now. There was no rush as there seemed to be little effect on their way of life. Tadeusz was his usual inattentive self but always treating Maria with respect. The balance had worked for years and had not really changed at all. Even during these recent weeks.

They finished their coffees in silence. Both reflecting on the same questions, but entirely different scenarios. They could not be further apart in their thoughts.

The hotel was full. Bookings were coming in for every week throughout the summer. Maria knew they would be busy. Tadeusz increased his time in his shed preparing his tools to do the odd jobs that kept him from under Maria's feet.

Two weeks followed way too slowly for his liking. Every day dragged. Maria kept giving him small tasks which kept him busy. But nothing seemed to take his mind off the letter that he hoped would arrive soon. He would go to meet Frank, their postman, every morning with anticipation. He had worked out how long his letter would take to get to Ella. How long for her to reply and post her letter back. The time he had worked out had come and gone. The reply was overdue in his mind. Tadeusz was now questioning what he had said in his letter. Or had Ella shared her secret with her husband, Witold? Perhaps the reply had been misdirected or even lost? Tadeusz explored every scenario to find a solution as to why his letter had not yet arrived.

Then on Saturday morning Frank arrived early with the post. He knew by now that Tadeusz had been expecting something which seemed very urgent. So, he grinned as he approached the end of the drive.

'Hi Tad,' he called. 'I think your letter is here – it's the foreign one, right?'

Tadeusz leapt forward grasping the bundle of post. He tried to change the subject as he didn't want Frank to start chatting about overdue or foreign post!

'Thanks, Frank. Yes, it's an old relative from the home country,' Tadeusz replied.

Frank nodded wisely. But he wasn't convinced, as he remembered the way in which Tad had snatched letters from Maria a couple of weeks before. His 30-odd years on the post beat had taught him about the importance of certain letters which brought vital information of all kinds. He was often amused about the odd neurosis expressed by his customers on his round. Anyway, he had delivered the bundle, so he waved goodbye to Tad and started his march back up the long drive.

Tadeusz was controlling his breathing. He knew his adrenaline was up again. He had to find a peaceful place to read this letter. So, he strode off towards his shed. Maria rarely went there as she didn't want to disturb Tadeusz's space and she really did not have any interest in his tools... He went in, sat down on his favourite stool and paused. *Goodness,* he thought. He now realised that he had been really stressed about the time it had taken for him to receive her reply. From his Ella, the woman he had loved so much so many years ago. He was slightly giddy in anticipation. Slowly he opened the letter. No need to rush now.

CHAPTER 10

M *y dearest darling Tadeusz,*

I was so moved by your affection and tenderness in your reply. It was beyond anything I could have hoped that you would write. I read with sorrow how your experiences in the war affected your memories. How the time eroded your links back to the life that we had planned to share for the rest of our lives. I realised that for you it was so much more difficult to remember the past. That every day away from your beloved parents, from your Warszawa and from me were days which slowly erased your entire previous life. And to read that you could only think of survival? I wept again and again when you described how you had to focus on that slender grasp on life itself. How you lost friends on a daily basis. How you had to force your way forward to reach for a new world. I sat for some time trying to absorb the colossal scale of you, your friends and our people, away from their country, with little hope of ever returning home.

My darling Tadeusz, I can so feel the pain in your letters. And in a strange way, I understand why you felt you had to explain what happened. And why you never came back to me in Warszawa. I really do understand now how it all unfolded for you during those horrendous years at war.

I went back and read your first reply to me and realised how difficult it must have been to open your heart again. To go back in time. To our time. And to discover how you really felt after all these years. We have both lost our entire lives together. And now I have found you in the latter years of our lifetime, it feels comforting to talk to you about what could have been. Perhaps most important for me has been the realisation of why you did not come back. To understand what happened to you during these many years. And why I found you in England. It could have been anywhere in the world?! But now you have described your life with your Maria, I can see how awkward it must have been to receive my original letter, from your first love...

I have been thinking about us and how we have both spent these past years. You with Maria and me with Witold. Both of us happy and content raising our respective families. For me there was always a piece of my heart that was locked forever, and it contained you. Your being right there. I think that because I did not experience the traumas that you endured, I just enveloped our relationship in hope. The hope that somehow you would eventually return. After the war. Then when you did not, I came to the eventual conclusion that you must have perished. So, I had to move forward and consider my own life without you. But I soon knew that it would never be like that... without you. I kept you with me and in the earlier years, I found myself chatting to you about us, our dreams and what might have been.

Even when I met Witold, I kind of told him about you and me. And he understood. He had also lost a close friend who had perished in the bombings of the city. So, he was not difficult or envious of our love. He rather offered to replace the void that you had left in me. We eventually got married and very soon started our journey with children. We were both in the legal profession and we worked as barristers in two different law firms in central Warszawa. Our lives were without much incident as our family grew. You can imagine as eventual judges we had to maintain a pretty steady existence and that extended to our sons, all of whom wanted to be lawyers as well. Three of them managed to qualify for the bar but two of them decided to turn to business using their legal experience.

Please tell me more about you and how your life developed in England, a completely strange country to you. How did you cope? How did you deal with earning enough to give your family any kind of start without the skills of being a lawyer? I need and would like to absorb the realities which you faced…

The curious fact is that my life evolved exactly as we had frequently discussed when we shared our ambitions back in those early years. And when I look back, I realise, especially now, that I had steered our life to be as we had planned. It meant that I could be closer to you, to us. Building a life which resembled our dreams. Is that awful of me to say that to you? I hope that this devotion which I am expressing is not too overwhelming? I have reached a new level of honesty with you that allows me to tell you how my life has been these past 30 years. In all honesty, I am learning things about my feelings simply by writing to you. No longer a ghost but a very real and live love of my life. My entire life.

I know my reply to you would have taken a little longer, but I had to think long and hard about my next question to you. And please be honest with your reply. I will be fine with your answers as I already am slightly afraid to even ask the question…

Do you think there is any way in which you could ask

Maria to allow you to come back to Poland and meet me? Just for one and only meeting?

I know it would be crazy to do this as we both have lives to which we have committed… and I realise that there is little future in such a meeting. But somehow, I feel that we must meet. That we are owed that meeting. Our lives were snatched from us by the fates of war. Surely now it would be reasonable to ask for that small request?

I have sat and thought about this for some days. Nothing else in fact as I had a few days' leave. So, my brain was filled with the opportunity and the implications. And my heart burst with excitement. To really consider that one day you and I could look at each other again. To allow our eyes to meet. And to let that physical contact wash over us just once more.

I had to pause to catch my breath, when writing this question. I am just too scared that you might say 'no'. That you would find all the right and logical reasons why it would not be appropriate or helpful for us to meet. I am besides myself with the possibility of meeting you again in Warszawa.

If you thought, we could… Please consider that we could! Then I imagined that we would meet in the famous Bazyliszek restaurant where we had planned to have our reception back then. I then imagined that you join me at the table. I would not need your photograph as I would know your spirit when you walk into the restaurant. I would dream of such a meeting... I yearn for it. Please consider it for both of us. It would complete our lives. And I could continue with my existence, happy in the knowledge that I touched your hand. And gently stroked your kind and beautiful face again. I sit here and sigh thinking that we are only two decisions away from making this possible...

Can you imagine, my darling Tadeusz? Can you imagine us meeting just once more? I leave you with that question. Probably the single most important question of my life. My heart is in your hands. Please tell me if this can be possible?

My deepest love to you, my darling Tadeusz.

CHAPTER 11

It was a bombshell. He really had to re-read the letter to even begin to grasp the enormity of the question. He had loved the early part of the letter. The fact that Ella really understood why he had not been able to find a way back to Warszawa. A way back to her, his beloved whom he had left behind. He loved reading about her feelings again, expressed in a different way but still full of the passion that had touched him from the very first letter.

But this new question? Really? How would that be even vaguely possible? He would have to tell Maria everything. About the letters. About his feelings. How it had affected him receiving these letters from Ella. It terrified him to even consider it. But behind that deep fear burned the start of a small desire. It had started with an unlikely spark when he first read the latter part of the letter. About the question.

Now two days had passed. Not much sleep. More wandering around looking vague. Tadeusz was just too beside himself with the potential answer to Ella's question. Could he go? How would he raise it with Maria? Did he have the right to ask? Where would he even start? It had the makings of a real affair which so far had been imagined. But to meet physically, well that would be a whole new question to answer.

Another three days went by. By now Maria thought Tadeusz had been suffering from a serious problem which he was not sharing with her. His behaviour had been erratic. Maria was confused but also upset. Tadeusz had always shared his problems with her. And she had most times been able to help solve them. Even when he had a scare with bowel cancer a few years before, Maria was able to keep Tadeusz calm through the ordeals of the treatments. Maria had looked after him and consoled him as much as he had needed.

Yet now Tadeusz was entirely closed. Nothing

mentioned. All very odd. Maria decided it was time to confront her man. What on earth was going on? That was the broad question for the evening over supper.

Tadeusz decided that tonight he would reveal the reasons for his strange behaviour. By now he knew that Maria was not entirely convinced that all was well. He knew that he could not keep any more secrets. The entire saga had gone too far. He had to find a way to discuss it with Maria. To reveal at least some of his feelings and then to consider how he would broach the question asked by Ella. He even decided that he may never ask the question depending on Maria's reactions to the revelation of the letters.

The reality in his mind was that he knew that he never wanted to lose Maria. Not under any circumstances. He had loved her with all his heart, without conditions, most of his adult life. So, he knew that the question could be only be answered by Maria. Only she could make the final decision. Without Maria's blessing it could never happen.

Now Tadeusz was overwhelmed. He knew that tonight was the night he would reveal as much as was reasonable. Maria had been too quiet these past days.

He knew that she would soon confront him if he did not open the subject himself.

Tadeusz organised for Angela, a local barmaid he had met working in a pub some 10 years before, to sit behind the bar for their guests. Maria liked Angela as she was a really nice young lady, but at the same time was firm with the customers.

Maria had been cooking supper for about an hour when Tadeusz walked in with a bottle of their favourite red – a dry Macon. He took down two glasses without speaking and poured them each a healthy sized glass of wine.

Maria knew this ritual. They were about to talk, and Tadeusz wanted to talk. *At last,* she thought, *I am about to find out what is going on.* Maria continued to stir the goulash, Tadeusz's favourite. They sat in silence for a few minutes and then he started.

'Well…' he launched in. 'As you probably have gathered, my darling, I have had something on my mind recently. Perhaps I have been acting peculiarly…'

Maria raised her eyebrows in that knowing way and looked him full in the face. He blanched. This was not starting as he had intended. But he continued as he could not hold back much longer. Regardless of which way it went for him.

'I got a letter from Poland a few weeks ago which was a shock to say the least. When I first saw the stamps, I thought it was from a distant relative. Well it sorts of was… Actually no, that's not correct.'

Again, Maria turned and looked at him witheringly, as if to say – 'get on with it as you're already way off the truth.'

'I don't know if I mentioned to you that back then in Poland, before the war, I was engaged to be married… I think I mentioned it but—'

Maria interrupted: 'Yes, to Ella.'

Tadeusz looked up with the look of a beaten man. Maria had even remembered her name. *Not going well at all,* he thought.

'Yes, Ella. That's right. Well Ella wrote to me. She told me she thought that I had died and discovered that I was alive!!' he blurted. Not in the way he had intended to explain the background at all! 'So, she wrote. To find out if it was me! Extraordinary that she found me. Found us,' he quickly added.

Maria continued to stare at him, listening intently.

Absorbing every movement of Tadeusz's face. Looking for the clues beyond the words spoken.

Tadeusz assumed that Maria's silence meant that he was to continue. So, he did.

'Anyway, she told me how she had tracked me, us. Told me about her husband and five children!! Can you imagine five children. All sons. Amazing!' he exclaimed, looking for any kind of approval from Maria. It was not forthcoming.

Maria turned to the stove and took the saucepan to the table in silence. She served two ample portions of goulash. Then added the rice. All in silence. Tadeusz studied her nervously but couldn't detect anything at all. *Women are so bloody good at this,* he concluded. He felt numb; not sure what to say or do next. *Keep calm,* he assured himself.

Maria sat down. She looked up enquiringly, as if to say 'continue'. Tadeusz launched into the next part of his speech though clearly not very well prepared.

'Anyway, it was a real shock to get the letter. I wrote back telling her how lovely it was to hear from her after all these years. I told her about you and me. About our time and how we met in the war, and how we are now living very happily in Bournemouth…'

He was reasonably convincing. Maria knew he was struggling. And now it all fell into place. The weeks of odd behaviour. The deep-thinking sessions. The fidgeting. All now was clear as a bell. Maria smiled inwardly. She decided that he must have worried himself silly when writing back, so she decided to be a little helpful…

'That's so amazing that Ella found you. Quite incredible after 37 years… What an extraordinary turn of events for both of you…' Maria smiled knowingly. Tadeusz looked drained but relieved that she had at least understood the letters.

'So, after you wrote and told Ella all about us and how lovely it is in Bournemouth, did she write back again? As I seem to remember that this all started quite a few weeks ago.'

Tadeusz detected a slightly sardonic note to Maria's question. But he ploughed on regardless.

'Yes, she wrote back just when I was planning to tell you. I have to be honest that I now wish I had not kept it to myself. As I always knew that I would tell you eventually. But it was all very tough to absorb. I didn't know what I thought about the letters. I was not sure whether I should reply and if I did, what I should say. But my darling I can tell you that I am glad that you know. It's been killing me to have kept it from you.'

Tadeusz looked down and breathed slowly. He was so relieved. Whatever the consequences, he wanted Maria to know. She deserved to know.

'Ella just wrote more of the same. How delighted she was to have found me. Us! And told me about her life now. She's a judge would you believe?!' he said enthusiastically. A little too glowingly, he realised.

'And how do you really feel about her contact with you now?' Maria asked in a flat tone. 'I am not going to quiz you about these past weeks of your behaviour as I doubt you even know what you were really thinking. But I do know it affected you. Possibly affected you a great deal.' Maria looked down and quietly added: 'And, with hindsight, I have to say that I'm a little disturbed about how much it might have touched you. To get letters from your ex-fiancée?'

Tadeusz poured another glass of wine for each of them. He pondered how best to answer. He knew

Ella had touched him deeply. Really reached inside and pulled him inside out. So now he had to confront the realities. What to say and what not to say. He was so bothered about not deceiving Maria, but he also knew it would be way too painful to share the full truth of the letters.

He turned to Maria and slowly started with his explanations: 'It did touch me. How could it not? I was engaged to be married to her. Before I had even met you. Our time during the war was a crazy time. We met. We fell in love. Our days were numbered. But we laughed at the stresses of war. We were together planning our future. Even though we did not necessarily believe we would survive. Our whole being was about survival. But with Ella, it was all laid out in front of me. Both parents ready and delighted. So, when the letter came, I started to drift back. Those times. The promises made...' Tadeusz put his head in his hands. He was tormenting himself with his explanations. He believed in the letters. And he believed in his life with Maria too. He looked up at her, searching for a sign of sympathy. But it was not yet forthcoming. Maria needed to understand more before she yielded to her man.

'I do understand, Tadeusz. Yes, I really do. I have listened to all you have said. And I've listened to what you have not said. It's a puzzle that I have yet to assemble.'

Maria paused. Tadeusz was about to blurt on with his explanations, but Maria held up her hand.

'I listened to you. And I didn't interrupt. So please stop now. Let me consider carefully what I am about to say.' Again, Maria looked down at the floor, to compose herself. She knew that what she was about to say would be difficult for her man to answer.

Maria got up and cleared the dishes. Tadeusz watched her intently. For any clues. He followed her around the kitchen helping clear the crockery into the dish washer. He was perplexed about what was about to come next. But he was also strangely calm, as he hoped that this evening's conversation would at least enable them both to find a way forward together...

Eventually Maria sat down. Tadeusz followed her to the table, and still watching her face for any expression which might tell him how she felt.

'Tadeusz, there are a few things that I find really

disconcerting. Even deeply upsetting. I am going to ask you the questions, but I don't want you to answer tonight. I want you to consider your answers until you are ready to tell me with complete honesty. It will be more important to me that you are totally honest with your feelings so that we can both consider the implications.'

Tadeusz, by this time, was wide-eyed. He had not expected such a clinical assessment of their situation caused by these letters. He had expected her to be anything from puzzled to perhaps angry. So, he sat in silence waiting for the questions.

Maria had been quiet for a few minutes, and then looked up at him, with tears streaming down her cheeks. She brushed them away as she didn't want any sympathy from him. Not now. She needed to be strong. It was not yet time for them to start hugging and crying. Too much was left, yet to be explained and defined.

'I have to ask you, Tadeusz, first, how is it possible that you kept these letters secret? I can understand the first letter was a shock. But to receive three letters and write back yourself, before saying anything to me? That has really hurt me deeply. Mostly because I don't understand why it needs to be secret.'

Tadeusz started to answer, but Maria stopped him firmly again with her raised hand. 'Please!' she said. 'I have told you that these questions cannot be answered now or today. You need to reflect on the real answers.'

Maria choked back a sob and continued: 'And secondly, when you have answered the first question to yourself, it will perhaps tell you the answers to my second question…'

Maria stopped again, bracing herself. She had to be firm, she told herself. Now was not the time to be soft or crying.

'How do you now really feel about Ella? Now that she is back in your life? In our lives? With our family? Please consider this carefully as I don't want to be massaged with a clever noncommittal answer. I need to know how you really feel about her words to you. Were they magical? Did they stir your affection for her? Did you find your love returning for your Ella? Are you now a little confused about us?'

Now Maria could not hold back the sobs. These

questions had thrown her life into turmoil. She had not a clue what had happened to her beloved man. And she knew the strength of a returning love would be huge. Especially as they had not broken up! No, they were about to married and had been deeply in love. Back then.

Tadeusz leaped forward to embrace her, but Maria shrank away. He persisted and put his arms around her. Maria submitted, but without responding. They sat there silently; both consumed with their own thoughts, neither being sure what the other was thinking. Right there and then.

Maria refused to let him have this moment. As if they had reached an affectionate few minutes to help the situation. Maria knew instinctively that to fight for her man, she had to ensure that he knew what was at stake. Nothing in the past 30 years had ever touched their relationship. They were completely happy with each other. And always in love. So, Maria knew that he had to consider the real answers so that he could arrive at the right conclusions and not drift on with his fantasy.

Maria had already concluded, that these letters

were a huge lift to his ego. A man, having reached the autumn of his life, to get letters from a previous love, would be glowing with a quiet pride. Nevertheless, she wanted him to not only stop his fantasy but also arrive at the right answers himself. It would be the only way back to her heart and forgiveness.

Maria got up. She smiled down at him. She gently stroked his face. And nodded at him with a smile. As if to say 'you know what you must do'.

'I am off to bed. Get some sleep, Tadeusz. It's late.'

He didn't move. He felt lost. Not sure what to say or how to respond.

'Yes, thanks. You too,' he replied lamely with almost a whisper.

He sat there. Poured himself another glass of wine. Not that he needed it, but he wanted to sit and think more. Not go to bed yet.

Everything Maria had said made sense to him. And he had long ago decided that not to have said anything sooner, had not been a good idea. He had messed up badly. His behaviour suggested that it was a secret and potentially a 'virtual' affair. Now what? He knew the answer to the first question – yes, he did want to keep his conversation private. After all he was looking at getting closure for both him and Ella. He could not do that when sharing the words with his Maria. This had to be a private conversation. Or so it had seemed at the time…

As to the second question, he had always maintained to himself that he was totally dedicated to his Maria and his family. Maria came first without question. He had been in love with Maria since the war and that love had grown without limits. So why was he now flirting with the notion of sharing such affectionate conversations with Ella? In his letters, he had expressed a lot of affection and even love to his Ella…

Tadeusz experienced a hot flush. He knew that this was now really much more of a mess than he had possibly realised. And typically, his Maria had nailed the exact two questions which would straighten the matter, or not.

Tadeusz decided that he had to be honest and not to be embarrassed about his feelings for his ex-fiancée. After all, his time with Ella had all happened before he had ever met Maria. Except that what had happened then was fine. This situation was about now. He shook his head, wondering how on earth he could justify what he thought were perfectly reasonable responses to a person who was so important in his life over 30 years ago.

His head drooped. Heavy with his thoughts. And not making much constructive progress. The problem was that he knew Maria was right but all the time he felt he also had his rights... He had a headache. No new thoughts. So, Tadeusz laid his head on the sofa arm just to rest a while. He did not feel he had the right to disturb Maria as at least an hour had gone by since she had left the living room.

Maria woke up at 3am with a start. She realised that Tadeusz had not come to bed. So, she put on her silk dressing gown and wandered off towards the living room. The light was still on. Tadeusz was lying awkwardly on the sofa and slightly snoring as his head was perched upwards on the sofa arm. Maria coaxed him to sit up on the sofa. She put a pillow behind his head and threw a blanket over him. He murmured something inaudible but was deep in sleep. Maria switched off the light. And then she stood there in the dark looking at her man. How much she loved him. She needed him back in her life. But she knew it would be a delicate battle to win him back, as he had to help himself. The decisions had to be his own. She left the room and returned to bed. But there was too much racing in her head to get any meaningful sleep.

The next morning, Tadeusz awoke with a start. It was 9.15am. Way too late for him. He was normally up at 6am to meet that wretched postman! *Oh, my goodness,* he thought. He had a shower and shave, using the time to gather his thoughts again. He had a plan, but he knew it had to be based on open honesty. That would be tough; but it was not negotiable. Maria had made it clear, and Tadeusz knew that Maria would know what the truth was, and what was manipulation of the thinking.

Tadeusz walked into the kitchen quietly. He came up behind Maria and bent down to kiss her neck as he said, 'Good morning.'

She did not resist and replied, 'Good morning. How did you sleep on the sofa?'

'Oh, it was fine,' he offered lamely. 'Thank you for giving me a blanket and pillow,' he said, smiling. It had not escaped him that Maria had bothered with him during the night. He felt that the small gesture was a positive omen.

Maria didn't answer but he saw her nod her head in response.

Maria had just finished feeding the squirrels. So, Tadeusz made the coffee and opened the bran flakes which they sometimes enjoyed together. They settled down to breakfast in silence. There did not seem to be anything they could say other than return to the conversation that they had the night before.

Tadeusz opened the dialogue first. 'Is Janine sorting the rooms without you this morning?'

'Yes,' Maria replied, turning to him as if to say that he needed to speak. Time to sort this mess.

Tadeusz tried a smile, but it was a weak gesture. So, he decided to launch in with his words, albeit unprepared.

'My darling, first and above all other words, I need to tell you that you are the most important person in my entire life. I am the luckiest man alive to have you in my life, sharing our years together. Nothing could ever turn me away from that fundamental belief in you. In us.'

He paused. He had not realised that it was his turn to have tears running down his cheeks. So, he wiped them away. Maria smiled supportively but did not move. In her mind, it was still way too early to share any signs of affection or love.

Tadeusz continued: 'So I need to repeat that it's important, you know and trust, that you are my one and only love and the most important person in the world to me.

'You asked two questions. The first was, why did I not share it with you when the letter first came? The answer is that I have no real idea. Actually, that's not strictly true. I think I wanted to understand it myself before I shared it with you. What do I mean by that? It was such a shock. And an intrusion into our lives. But an intrusion from someone I knew so well. Suddenly in my mind, I concluded that she had every right to intrude. She simply wanted to say that she had found me. That she was thrilled I was alive. All of which was fair – as you already said to me. It's my reaction to keep it a secret that you question. And I believe it was because the contents of the letter were from the only person in the world who could intrude. It was as if she was making an affectionate claim on me. And I did not know how to deal with that claim. She expressed her love but only based on the past. When we were torn apart. She told me how much she loved her husband and her boys. So, she wanted me to understand that she was not in fact making any demands on me, or my feelings. But she did want me to know how much she had always loved me and always will love me until the day she dies.'

Tadeusz looked up at Maria pleadingly. As if to say: 'I cannot do this alone.' He was wiping away his tears. He felt he had been honest in his summary. Maria smiled but urged him to continue without any response from her.

'So, I wrote back to her. I told her that I was thrilled to hear from her. I told her how my life had moved on during the war. How I met you and built a new life in England. And I told her how much I loved you, my darling, and our family. But I did tell Ella that I loved her too.'

He again looked up at Maria. Now she had tears. But he carried on.

'Yes, I do love her, my darling. But I am not in love with her. And I am very deeply in love with you. I can only ask that you understand why I have to love that person with whom I had promised to build a life in Poland. For a while, yes, I did indulge myself but that was just my ego. I was quite pleased that this person from my past had such affection for me, based on our being engaged to be married. But I have thought a lot about your question, and I believe I kept it from you for personal reasons as I did not think I could tell you how I might feel about Ella as a person from my past.'

Tadeusz reached forward and held Maria's hand. They had always believed in the touch of their hands together. He enveloped it with a gentle squeeze. Maria squeezed back and then withdrew, still wanting the answer to the second question.

Tadeusz leaned back as if to draw breath. He had already partly answered the second question, but he knew Maria would need a conclusive answer.

Maria held her breath for a minute. She was so relieved and thrilled to hear his words. They were honest. And their love seemed to be intact. Still as one. She turned to him and tilted her head. 'Tadeusz do you want to continue, or do you want me to respond?'

Tadeusz looked at her warm face and decided to continue. He wanted to get to the end and also to ask the last question. He knew he had to ask today as he would never ask another time.

'I'm OK,' he said. 'Yes, I would like to carry on as I have cleared my head as well, I think I can.'

'How do I feel about Ella? I have already told you that I do love her. For the simple reason that one day, long ago, I was promised to Ella, to spend my life with her. That day passed. And I found you. The circumstances were strange with us meeting during the war. But when I met you, I was a fallen man. I knew that we had always been destined to be together. And that feeling has never left me.'

He paused. And then continued.

'Yes, the simple answer is that I was really pleased to hear from Ella. It was probably because I never had thought about the fact that we had all moved in our lives. But without closure with Ella. So, I did tell her that of course I loved her, but I should have added that not in that way that I love you. I was not in love with her and I failed to say that.'

At last he felt that he had said it. The truth. He had actually realised the words as he spoke them. It tumbled out at the end without any rehearsal of thought.

Maria nodded and understood. She leaned forward and took his hand again. 'Thank you, Tadeusz. That was the truth. Some of it painful but the truth.'

She looked at his face, but she detected that there was more, and that they had not arrived at the final hurdle yet. She gave him a hug but then sat back as if to say that she knew that there was more to say.

Tadeusz was grateful for the hug, as he needed fortification for the last question not yet mentioned.

'Now the last question is simple, but it came from Ella.'

Maria raised her eyebrows. This she did not expect. What on earth was coming now? She braced her shoulders and faced Tadeusz with a renewed strength. Maria had won the day. She was calm. And now she would not give up her man any further.

Tadeusz seemed calm too, although his pulse was

in full flow.

'In her last letter, Ella wondered if there was any chance of my coming over for one last supper together in Warszawa, and would you have any objections to that?'

Maria's mouth dropped open.

'Before you reply, I can tell you that that I am fine with either answer. It's entirely up to you.' He smiled helpfully.

Maria stopped smiling. She had to think about this quickly as she knew that the answer was much more critical than seemed obvious. She got up and lit a cigarette and looked out of the window. Tadeusz watched her every move. He knew it was a ridiculous question, but he had promised Ella that he would ask. And deep down he knew that he would like to go, just for this one last time to meet with Ella.

Maria knew that both answers were loaded against her. If she said that she preferred that he didn't go, then it would stay with them for the rest of their lives. Maria would be the woman who stopped her husband from getting closure. After all, it had not been their fault that the war had torn them apart. How could she stop that? It would seem so unreasonable. And now, especially after Tadeusz had declared his undying love, how could she deny him this question? Or more a request?

Tadeusz understood her confusion and the dilemma she was facing. He started to think that he should withdraw the question as he could not ruin what he and his beloved had achieved in the face of this mess.

Then Maria turned and with a strong smile said: 'Of course you must go, my darling. You both deserve this closure you seek. That you need.'

And she stepped across the room to Tadeusz and grabbed his huge body in her small arms and crushed him to her. She sobbed a little but was also smiling. He turned her face up to him and asked: 'Are you sure, my darling Maria? You really are OK with this?'

'Yes. I am sure. Of course, I am.' And she continued to hold him in a massive hug.

They sat down together and started to discuss a plan. Maria took an active interest, as she knew she had to be involved, to protect her man from losing his way.

And Tadeusz had found his way to get closure with Ella, and all with the blessing of his beloved Maria.

That night they went to bed slightly drunk. As they had supper with two bottles of wine. Giggling together for hours. Maria was making sure that he was totally in love in his mind, but only with her.

CHAPTER 12

The next morning, they both woke early, each nursing a small headache. Maria was up first as she had work to do in the hotel. Tadeusz lurched onto his side and closed his eyes. The evening before was slowly coming back to him. He gradually started to remember the long discussions, the emotions and the words Maria used at the end.

He was exhausted with the talking about Ella and the letters. At one point he genuinely thought that perhaps all had been lost, as his deception did amount to a considerable shift in Maria's trust in him. But he also knew that their time together during the night was very real and genuine. He aimed to build on that time. He desperately wanted to get back to the affection and love they had shared all of these years.

But now he had Maria's agreement that he should go to Poland, at last, to meet with Ella. He could barely conceal his excitement. To go back to his beloved country. To be amongst his people. To smell the fragrances of Warszawa. And above all, to see his Ella again, for one last time. He knew he could only go once. But once would be enough.

He decided to write to Ella tomorrow. He needed to spend time with Maria, to share the work and to be with his love.

Tadeusz went through to the kitchen to find Maria. She was just stacking the plates, when she felt his hand on her arm... She turned towards him with a smile.

'Well that was a special night?' he offered, with a slight question in his tone.

'Yes, it was.' Maria smiled again. 'So, when will you be going?' she asked. 'What plans will you make?' Maria wanted to be part of the whole process, to avoid any secrecy. The only way forward for her now was to be positive and supportive, despite her misgivings. In her heart she was still concerned that this was not a healthy solution. How would he be with her? What old emotions would it stir? Could he see her one more time and then forget? These questions circled in her mind, constantly occupying her thinking… to the extent that she could not really focus on her hotel chores. *It will get better,* she reassured herself.

'I thought maybe I will write tomorrow afternoon, when it's quiet in the hotel. And then to organise the trip soon. I am not sure it would be good for us both if this was much delayed. What do you think, my darling?' he replied.

Maria nodded in agreement. Not saying anything at this stage. Let Tadeusz do what he thinks best. Tadeusz took her assent as confirmation that he should go ahead and get it done. He helped her with clearing the food away after their lunch. Maria went to sort out Janine the cleaner, while Tadeusz retired back to his desk to deal with the bookings.

What an extraordinary few weeks they had lived through together. He couldn't really focus on his papers. So, he laid down, for an afternoon nap. Trying not to think about his impending trip to Poland.

Goodness knows he was so excited. Any trepidation had now left his mind, as he drifted off into sleep.

Maria wondered if there was anything else she could do maintain some grasp on his plans. So that he did not disappear again. Men were so easily led despite all best intentions, she thought. At one point, she toyed with the idea that perhaps she could join him. Not to be there for his meeting but go under the pretext that she would also like to visit her homeland again. It seemed a perfectly reasonable idea. And not one that he could easily resist in her view. The idea grew in her mind, but when would she suggest it to him? He was already planning to write to his Ella tomorrow. She would think about it and maybe discuss at supper. That seemed to her the best idea, before he wrote the letter.

The day drifted by. Tadeusz woke around 4pm. His head was still groggy from the previous night's drinking. He got up unsteadily and shuffled over to the bathroom. He would not be drinking again tonight, as he needed his head to be clear for his letter. Ella would not believe it! That he would be actually coming to see her? Impossible! Tadeusz got excited all over again, but he knew that he had to maintain a calmness as being excited would not do at all.

Maria had organised a light supper, which passed without comment. Just towards the end when they were gathering up the plates, Maria dropped her small bombshell.

'Tadeusz. I've been thinking… would you mind very much if I came with you? Not to meet with Ella, of course, but to use the time to visit Warszawa. See some relatives and just enjoy returning to Poland? I assume that you plan to go for one night only, so we could maybe make a weekend of it together?' Maria held her breath for his answer.

Tadeusz was aghast. This he had not allowed for in any of his thinking about the trip. He paused and replied: 'Yes, of course that would be wonderful.' He turned towards her and smiled with an air of confident confirmation. Maria watched intently. She knew every line and expression in his face. There was little he could hide from her. So, she held his gaze but did not add any words. This tactic unnerved Tadeusz as he had no idea where to take the conversation. Nor did he have a clue about how the trip would work if Maria came with him. Fortunately, his friend Stefan was at the bar for his last evening before going back to London. Tadeusz extracted himself with an apology and hurried off to the bar before Maria could speak any more about his trip. In fact, Maria had no intention of continuing with the idea, as she knew this had to rest with Tadeusz for now.

Tadeusz arrived in the bar, with a slightly flushed expression. Stefan was already there, reading the local newspaper. He looked up and said: 'Hi, Tadeusz. What's the hurry? Are you OK?'

'Sure,' replied Tadeusz. He spun around to the bottles and started to pour Stefan's favourite drink, a gin and tonic. He poured himself a glass of red, as always.

'I'm going,' he offered.

'Going where?' said Stefan. Tadeusz looked at him with a look that said this was not an ordinary conversation but an appendix to the chat they had at the beginning of the week.

'Oh, my word. Really?' asked Stefan. 'You told Maria? You told her everything? And she agreed to you going? That is a surprise!'

'What's a surprise?' asked Tadeusz confidently, as if to say that it was perfectly normal. He had already forgotten the anxieties that he had expressed to Stefan only a week ago. Or maybe not forgotten but smoothed over, now that he had received permission to go.

'Yes, I did tell her everything, as you suggested,' he said gruffly. 'Your words were good advice. I knew I had to tell her everything, but you made sure that I did sooner rather than later. It was a tough conversation. We spent a long time talking. In fact, it continued over two nights before we got to the end.' He paused and looked down for a while.

Stefan raised his eyebrows, clearly impressed. He knew it could not have been an easy conversation. And now Tadeusz had even managed to organise that he could go back to the home country.

'Well I am impressed and so pleased for you, my friend. Sharing with Maria is one thing, but also then getting her agreement to go was a serious result for you.' Stefan smiled approvingly.

'She wants to come with me,' Tadeusz replied

blandly, as if it meant very little.

'What?!' Stefan exclaimed. 'How on earth will that work? Surely that's not an option if you are to meet Ella?' he continued.

'Well I don't think she means to be there with me when I meet Ella, but she asked if she could visit Poland too. Seemed like a reasonable thought.' Tadeusz spoke these words with as much conviction as he could muster. 'But to be honest, Stefan, I could do without the distraction. There is nothing for me to hide, and am sure it would be fine, but somehow it does not feel like this should be the time to visit Poland. Maybe we could do that together at another time.'

Stefan nodded in agreement. He couldn't help thinking that it seemed to defeat the point of the trip. But then he was thinking like a man and not at all like his very good friend Maria.

'Perhaps you should suggest that to her. Offering that you would only go for a quick trip, one night in Warszawa and back? Maybe suggest it would be a confusing trip and you both wouldn't want to spend the whole journey discussing the reunion with Ella?

Just deflect the reason for going...' Stefan was offering solutions but unconvincingly as he knew Maria to be a strong woman who was also very smart when it came to male manipulations of arguments.

But Tadeusz liked the line of thinking. It did make sense, and honestly it would be such a distraction to have Maria on the trip with him. He thought about Stefan's words. He might try that on Maria the next morning before he wrote his letter.

Stefan could see Tadeusz assembling the arguments in his mind. Well this had to be his battle and Stefan had no intention of siding with him. In case he bumped into Maria tomorrow morning, before leaving, and knowing her withering look. She would know that they talked tactics and she would know who sided with whom.

Tadeusz switched subjects and launched into his views about the ongoing Iron Curtain debacle. It did seem that Gorbachev was somehow looking at finding middle ground with the West. Stefan joined in, obviously relieved not to be asked for more advice. And so, they talked for another hour, before Stefan called it a night. He had a long drive back to London the next day. So, he wanted to be fresh. He bid goodnight to Tadeusz and gave him a hug. 'You will know what to do, my dear friend,' he added.

They both went off to their respective bedrooms. Tadeusz came into his room and Maria was already fast asleep. He was relieved as he still had not sorted his thoughts about them both going together to Poland. Or not.

The next morning Tadeusz was up at his usual hour. He went through to the kitchen and made two coffees for him and Maria. They could chat before they needed to get up and say goodbye to the departing guests.

He brought the coffee through and Maria was just sitting up and puffing up her cushion behind her back. They kissed with a little more effort than normal, obviously both wanting to show a stronger sign of affection. There was no doubt that the discussion might have finished on a good note, but it had left anxieties.

Tadeusz decided that he should float Stefan's argument to see if he could carry the trip to Poland alone.

'I was talking to Stefan last night, about my trip.'

'My trip or our trip?' she asked with an impish smile.

'Well, I was thinking that maybe if I am going for one night only, then it would be nicer for us both to go together in a few weeks' time. As I would want you to experience the same, and we could drop by via Poznan to visit with your family at the same time. What do you think?' He looked a little battle worn but still trying to be optimistic.

Maria looked down just for a moment before she turned her head to meet his gaze. 'Well, if you think that would be best then I am fine with that, Tadeusz, my darling.'

Is she being sarcastic? he thought. Was this a real submission to his plan or was there more to come? He had no idea what to say, so he sat still quietly nursing his cold coffee. What to do? What to say? He was clueless. Maria was so much better at these discussions.

'OK. So, you go and enjoy that two-day trip, and then we can go again in a few weeks. Good plan.'

Oh no! Again, he had no idea if this was part of a plan which would end in him being ridiculed or verbally beaten into submission. So, he decided to go with the direction taken by Maria and ignore any sub plots that were haring around in his head.

'OK. I will book my flights and also flights for us say in four weeks' time – depending on how we can organise the guests with our Janine in charge. What do you think?' he asked, although the tone was more of a statement than a question.

'Sure,' said Maria, with an air of a defeated woman. But secretly she knew that this pressure made it tougher for him to plan a marvellous or even semi-romantic trip. It would all be over in 48 hours. And then would come the reality. The reckoning. She would have to let him have his day with Ella in peace. And then would steer them back to the safety of their previous world. It was going to be a long time to get to normality but for now Maria had to be strong and keep her man on track.

'OK. I'm off to do my bookings. Are you OK with Janine?' he asked, absentmindedly. Maria started to get up to get herself started as it was almost 7.30am and there was a lot to do.

Tadeusz reached his desk and flopped down in his

old chair. Nearly there. He was now on the last track of an extraordinary journey. He felt very calm as he had genuinely consolidated his love with Maria, and she was entirely supportive. In his head it was now perfectly reasonable that he should be able to see his ex-fiancée this one last time. Everybody needed closure.

CHAPTER 13

M *y darling Ella,*
I so enjoyed reading your letter reply. I read it so
many times just to feel your affection across the space that
divides our two countries. I have so many questions to ask you
about you. About your new life with your family. It seems so
strange to be asking all these new things of you when we were so
close back then at the start of our lives. When we knew
everything about each other. So much to talk about. What is
worse, is not just the facts about you. About what you like?
But the real feelings beneath the surface about your life. We
used to discuss those deeper feelings when we walked and
talked. And now you have had a lifetime of them but alone.
Without me. So many years of feelings accumulated with others.
With your new family that we never shared together. That is

what I want to share with you now. To hear your stories. But no longer by letter, my darling.

I am coming to visit! Yes, I have agreed with Maria and all is to be fixed. How wonderful for us both that we can meet after all of these years??? I am so excited now that it is all agreed. I cannot wait to see you. To give you a huge bear hug. And to listen to you into the early hours. For I will only have one day and one night to share with you.

But let's not think about how much time we have. Let's think that we will have a little time together after all of these years. Time that was stolen from us by the war. And now, because you found me, we will have the comfort and peace that we have held hands one more time.

I have discussed it all with Maria and we had some deep conversations about it. I will not talk to you about my very loving relationship with Maria and you need not tell me about your Witold. I think we should just talk to each other about us and our history apart. That will be so very special for me.

Our hotel needs me most of the time but two days away is not a major problem. I can book the last two days of this month if that works for your diary, which I imagine is very busy. I would get into Warszawa on British Airways around 2pm and to my hotel by around 4.30pm. I know that this might be a little bizarre, but it would be wonderful if we could have a drink in the late afternoon in the open square. And then you could join me for supper to continue our conversations until it is time to cease and sleep. How does that plan appeal to you? Whatever we agree to do will be so exciting! I am almost shaking with anticipation at the thought of seeing you again, my dearest Ella. So much.

With Love.

Your Tadeusz

He decided not to make it a long letter this time. He had said what he wanted to say. The rest would be in person. The whole exercise took him no longer than 40 minutes. His soul was on fire. *Hold onto yourself,* he thought. He would see Ella and then come back to his Maria. A very complicated time over next two weeks. But he was sure that he understood what had to happen and how to manage himself. He sighed deeply. So excited.

He put the letter into an envelope and nipped out of the back door to go to the Post Office. He did not want another conversation with Maria. She could interrupt his flow and also may even ask to see his letter although, to be fair, he doubted that she would stoop to that tactic. He was soon down the road walking briskly, even excited again. The letter was soon stamped and went into the bag behind the window, marked "overseas". Tadeusz wheeled around and strode back to the hotel. He was trying to imagine how excited Ella would be to get his letter and to know that they would finally meet after so many years. He smiled to himself and kept that smile all the way back to the hotel.

His next job was to book the time out of the hotel. That would be OK as he had already checked the bookings and the last two days of May were fine. He would not be missed.

He sat down at his desk and called the travel agent. He checked flights to Warszawa and booked the two flights for those last two days in May. He then checked hotel availability at Julia's apartments in the Old Square, which is where he planned to meet Ella. He did not want a long way to walk at the end of their evening. Fortunately, there were two double-bedroom apartments left so he booked one with a view onto the Old Square.

He was in a daze. This was all going to happen, more than 35 years later. In the same Old Square where he had proposed to his Ella. His feelings were becoming so confused. He had to stop. This was not how he wanted to be when he went to Warszawa. He wanted to be happy but in control. And he was far from that.

The next days moved along very slowly. Tadeusz worked with Maria, but they did not discuss his impending trip. Maria was aware that Tadeusz was spending much more time with her and attempting to do much more than he normally did around the hotel. This behaviour amused her, as she knew it was typical of a man to massage the edges of a deal that they had struck. But equally she was concerned, as Tadeusz was different again. He seemed to be closer physically, but his mind was elsewhere. Obviously, he was already on a plane to meet his beloved Ella! That was not the plan in her mind, but she wanted to be a realist. He was bound to be excited. Maria concluded that this was not an affair but an attempt at closure… so he should be allowed to enjoy his meeting with Ella? Maria continued to try to justify the entire plan, but she did also have a sense of foreboding. The scariest part for Maria was that Tadeusz might recover many of his old feelings. That they would share so many of their previous dreams that it would be difficult to tear himself away from that prospect. So, Maria continued to run the hotel day by day. They continued to exchange pleasantries and issues about hotel bookings, but they did not return to the journey which was getting closer day by day.

Tadeusz tried hard to be as accommodating as possible. He knew that he had put his Maria under immense pressure, and she had been so generous in releasing him to go. He believed that he had an idea of what she was going through; but he assured himself that there was nothing to be concerned about. It had never occurred to him that Maria might not be the same person when he returned. He just believed in this journey and that Maria was going to support him throughout.

The last piece in this part of the puzzle was Ella's reply. He knew instinctively that Ella would be absolutely thrilled with the decision that he would come to meet her in their beloved Warszawa. But he needed the letter. The reply to confirm that it was OK at her end to meet with him. Again, he had not considered whether her husband Witold would be in agreement, like his Maria. So, Tadeusz was slightly anxious about receiving the next letter as the days moved towards his flight date.

It was only three days before the flight date that he got the reply. He was so relieved. And especially so that he managed to snatch the letter from the postman's hand and disappear into his study before Maria might get involved or even ask to see the letter… His blood ran cold. He really did not need that to happen.

Tadeusz darted to his desk and quickly opened the letter:

My darling Tadeusz,

I was so shocked and thrilled to get your letter! I cannot believe that I am going to see you again, my darling. There are no words which can possibly express my sheer excitement. From the second that I discovered that you were still alive, all I wanted to do was to slip into your strong arms and crush you against me. I want to hold your beautiful hands and stroke your handsome face. I am completely beside myself with the joy of seeing you here, in our City of Warszawa. I want to keep writing so many more words to tell you how I feel but I realise that now is not the time to do that. I am being allowed to do that to you in person which is so much more than I could have possibly hoped for. All those many years when I believed you were dead, and I mourned the loss of you, of us together. Then to find you alive and now am going to see you again?? It is beyond words. Thank you from the bottom of my soul.

You have not told me how Maria has taken this journey of yours. I know you told me that she is supportive but, as a woman, it cannot have been easy for her to agree. Was it so very difficult? I am sorry to pry but I am a woman and I understand how difficult your conversation must have been. Anyway, enough of my questions. I am sure you will tell me whatever you think is necessary. The most exciting thing in my whole life is about to happen in the next few days and that is enough for me. Now until the day I die. It will be enough.

Witold was very surprised and uneasy. It did not make much sense, but he knew he could not change the reality. He also understood that this is one thing in our lives that he must not block. There was nothing that could stop me seeing you if you were able to come. So, we agreed, and we have not discussed it since that night when I got your last letter.

I have now booked our old restaurant and know Julie's apartments in the Old Square. Please let me collect you at 7pm and we can stroll across the square together, arm in arm, a little like those days, back then, when we were in love, as one.

As I say these words, I cannot believe in them. The fact that this meeting is about you and me is completely surreal to me. Can it really be you and me, Tadeusz? Is this really going to happen? My heart is pounding just thinking of the moment I can hug you and not speak, until I have absorbed you into my soul. It is a matter of 6 days to the day when we meet so am going to go now to the post office and mail this as fast as they can carry to you in England.

My darling. We will soon be together. For one more time. I really cannot wait, and doubt if I will sleep at all for the next days until I see your beautiful face again.

I am sending you all of my deepest love.

From your Ella

Tadeusz dropped the letter on his desk as if it were on fire. His heart was thumping in his chest. He then quickly put it into his bottom drawer, not knowing what to do next. Ella had written with such deep feeling. And he felt every word imprint itself on his heart. How could Ella be so completely pure in her thoughts? He now really understood what this meeting meant to her, and to him. The memory of his youth was now fresh and back in his veins. He was going to meet his fiancée to talk about their love. And Ella had certainly expressed her limitless love to him in this last letter.

Tadeusz sat and pondered about his dilemma. For now, he felt a massive surge of guilt. He had promised Maria that this was simply a reunion, with his old friend and fiancée from before the war. It was to be a simple matter of closure for them both. Not one of expressions of deep love to each other! He had believed that he would be in control. Obviously, he knew that it would be an emotional encounter, but he also believed in what he had promised Maria. Her generous spirit to let him go with her blessing was very special. He knew it could not have been an easy decision.

Tadeusz stood up and went to the door of his study. He opened the door and peeped out into the corridor. Nobody there. He wandered down the corridor to check on hotel progress. Janine was cleaning the last of the rooms. He asked about Maria's whereabouts.

'She went to the supermarket,' Janine replied. 'Said she would be back in an hour or so.' Tadeusz nodded his thanks and silently slipped back to his study. Janine was surprised as he usually stopped to chat about local gossip when Maria was not around.

Tadeusz took out the letter again and read it a second time. More slowly so that he could really take in the passion. It was just so emotive. So pure and honest. He could feel the love in the words. The letter carried so much to him in England. Ella was there for him alone. Soon.

He realised that he had to let his guard down and be that person she was expecting. He could not go to Warszawa and be a distant friend or an old acquaintance. He had to be the person in whom she believed, the person who was her fiancé in those happy days before the war. Now life had moved on. It was 30 years since they had last seen each other. But they had been so in love. They had never even had an argument. It was pure romance. And Ella had said as much again in her letters after all these years. So, Tadeusz decided that he must now stop the guilt. He must face the reality of his journey to meet with his beloved Ella.

And then he would return to the woman of his life, Maria. And they would continue to live their lives as if nothing had happened. That was his plan and his decision to himself.

Tadeusz got up wearily. He was exhausted with thinking first one way and then the other. He wanted to see Maria and share a glass of wine. He would keep his plan from her, as there would be nothing to be gained from sharing his deepest thoughts.

Maria was walking back from the supermarket. Her thoughts had not been on much else. The day after tomorrow he would be gone. She would lose him for the next 48 hours and would have no knowledge of his feelings or how this meeting would go. But of course, she knew how it would go. Who was she kidding? Not herself surely? Maria knew that Tadeusz couldn't resist the temptation of this reunion with his beloved Ella. Not just the meeting, but the expressions of affection that would be swirling around during their heady encounter. Perhaps even more they might talk of their lost love. Maria's eyes brimmed with tears. She needed to control herself so that she was strong for Tadeusz. She didn't want him to know of her fears. Not now. She wanted him to go and find that his love for her, Maria, was so much stronger and based on so many happy years together. He had to go through this strange encounter and emerge from the other side, with his heart wholly given to their lives forever to the end of their days. That was the challenge for them both. Maria did flirt with the question of how she would be when Tadeusz returned. She pondered whether this could be a stain on their love. Would it be there always as a small wound which kept festering? The scars never to heal.

As Maria went over her feelings again and again, she arrived at the hotel. Tadeusz was at the door waiting to greet her. She pulled herself together with a snap. She didn't want any of this to become part of their conversation. It was only a few more days of pain and then gone. Or so she hoped.

Tadeusz smiled wanly. He offered to take the bags, which she allowed. They both walked to the kitchen side by side without talking. Eventually Tadeusz said: 'I got a letter from Ella confirming the arrangements so all good for me to go day after tomorrow.' He paused, looking for any reaction. Maria gave nothing away.

'Good,' she said. 'Do you want me to drive you to the airport?' she asked.

Tadeusz blanched. What should he say? Did he want that?

'Yes, that would be wonderful if you don't mind… It's a long way there and back!'

'That's fine,' she responded. 'I'm happy to do that for you.' She wondered why on earth she had offered as the journey would not be easy. She wished she had not offered, and Tadeusz felt the same. But neither wanted to explore other options. It was done and agreed.

They had supper together. Tadeusz opened a fresh bottle of red wine. And so, they shared that with mutual enthusiasm. Maybe a few drinks would take the edge off their last hours together. They chatted about the hotel again. Then they moved onto discussions about building a vegetable garden, which

Tadeusz said he would start as soon as he returned. They were building continuity together. As if they could gloss over the next 48 hours and get back to their lives together again. The conversation was a little stilted but got better as the copious wine took effect. They retired to bed together both smiling at each other. They were offering reassurance from both sides which seemed a good place to be. Maria switched off the bedside light and turned to Tadeusz. It was an impromptu feeling, but she felt he needed to go with more than a peck on his cheek. Maria reached for him and started their ritual of lovemaking. It was never hugely passionate. Those days had long gone. But it was full of affection and physical contact. Tadeusz always found it to be a powerful way to be close to his Maria. And this time they did seem to share more passion. Maria wanted him to know that she would be waiting for him. And that he belonged to her. They both finished with a long sigh and held each other longer than normal. She wanted him to feel her spirit. And he wanted her to believe in his love. After a few minutes of embracing they pulled away and both lay on their backs staring at the ceiling.

They felt slightly elated, as they had not made love for some months, but also a little uneasy. Tomorrow he would be gone.

The affection they shared the night before was still with them the next morning. They lingered near each other, both aware that the next two days could have a marked effect on the rest of their lives. But having both agreed that Tadeusz should go, it meant that they had to hold onto their emotions and keep things in check for now. The reality would unfold in its own way, and that would depend on both Tadeusz and Ella.

They drove to the airport in silence, occasionally chatting about the hotel. And then Maria brought up the subject of her visiting Poland when they could both go later in the year. Maria told Tadeusz that she would write to Kasia, her aunt living in Poznan, about the proposed trip. She said that they would be thrilled to see them all after all of these years. They had corresponded many times, but nobody had entertained much hope in the possibility of them seeing each other ever again. The Communists were not enthusiastic about visits from returning Poles. And it was only in recent years that visas were being issued, but always in a very controlled way. So, they drove on, talking of a trip to Poznan, but Tadeusz couldn't wait to get away and onto the plane. He found that their last moments together in the car to be deeply awkward. He needed to think about going home to Poland for the first time in 37 years.

They arrived at Heathrow after a two-hour drive. They had agreed that she would drop him rather than park. They were both relieved with that decision, as it was definitely time to let go. They got out and Tadeusz took his hand luggage from the boot. He put it on the floor. And turned to Maria. He held both of her shoulders with a gentle grasp and smiled at her reassuringly. Maria returned his smile, but her eyes were brimming with tears. She was furious with herself as she really did not want Tadeusz to recognise her fears. She was allowing her man to go to another woman for no other reason than history required it. She did not believe it was a good enough reason, but she had no choice. Tadeusz then grabbed her into a warm embrace, and they held each other for a few seconds, before she pushed him away with a shudder.

'Enjoy yourself, my darling. Please give Ella my

regards. And say hello to our homeland from me…'
With that, she turned and went straight to the driver's
door and got into the car. Maria briefly looked at him
and waved, as she started forward into the main
traffic lane. Tadeusz could barely wave back as he
held the luggage in one hand and passport with tickets
in the other. And then she was gone.

Tadeusz stared after the car. He was relieved but
also concerned. He knew why he should be
concerned but he was on his way. He steered himself
towards the British Airways departure counter and
eventually to the gate where the boarding had already
started. He quickly stopped at the cosmetic counter
and purchased a bottle of pure perfume. He chose
Chanel No. 5 – a classic and not one that his Maria
used. He wanted to have a small gift for Ella. He got
to his seat and sighed. His heart was pounding as he
was beyond excitement. Not only was he going to see
his Ella, but he was returning to his homeland. Where
he had been born and raised. Where everybody
around in every corner were all Polish. Not just the
occasional waitress in a café in Bournemouth, but
everywhere. He was just beside himself with joy.

CHAPTER 14

The plane journey seemed almost unreal. Tadeusz just could not believe that he was actually on his way. He stared out of the window, wishing the land underneath to pass by quickly. He took a small lunch as he had no appetite. His excitement was in charge of his being. And eventually he was rewarded, as the outline of his beloved Poland came into view. He had passed over Germany with strong emotions inside him. He hadn't thought much about this nation for some time, but it all came flooding back. These people had ravaged his country and ripped him, and so many millions of his country people away from their home.

But there was not time to dwell on the past. He was on his way back and only 30 minutes from landing in Warszawa airport. He could see his country beneath him. A huge warm glow came over him as he watched through the window. His shoulders gently shuddered with emotion. Tears fell freely down his cheeks. And eventually he smiled. Home at last. The plane landed smoothly. Tadeusz gathered his small case and shuffled along the corridors to Passport Control. He found it strange to have a British passport while watching many Poles going through their own exit. He felt almost like a foreigner. He got to the counter and the Polish officer greeted him in Polish. Tadeusz replied with huge enthusiasm. He had spoken Polish on his own soil. He walked through to the taxi rank, taking in the volumes of conversations all in his mother tongue. He had to stop and put down his case. He needed to just look around and take it in. The old familiar sounds. The ethnic displays. The airport was full of pretty girls with blonde hair and blue eyes. All smiling. He loved every moment. The welcome was so warm and natural.

He slowly ambled through to the taxi rank and asked the driver to take him to the Old Square. This was the Old Square where he had planned to marry his Ella. During the war the beautiful square with buildings dating back to 1600, had been destroyed by bombs. Destroyed beyond recognition. After the war, the Poles gathered together, and rebuilt the entire Square brick by brick to exactly replicate what had been there before. It was a famous and miraculous achievement. Polish pride was at stake and their Old Square was a tribute to their determination.

Tadeusz asked his driver to stop well before the destination, as he wanted to walk there slowly. To take in the old buildings and the beauty of the surrounding cobbled streets. The shops were full of old antiques and artefacts. Eventually he arrived at the edge of the square. Tadeusz simply broke down. It was just too much for him to bear. This was his home. He had eaten so many times here with his beloved parents. He had been drunk here with his student friends on the odd evening. And he had proposed to Ella right here in this stunning square. But he also smiled. This was his home and he was here at last. He had never ever though that this day would come. He had long ago given up on any such possibility. And now it had all happened in what seemed to be a matter of days. Gone were his doubts. He had already forgotten about the pain caused by speaking to Maria about coming. He walked across the square very slowly, gazing at the extraordinary buildings that looked exactly the same, despite having been rebuilt from the ground in 1946. He arrived at Julia's apartments and checked in. He got to his rooms with one final push and sat down on the bed, pretty exhausted with the entire ordeal. And as if that had not been enough, he allowed himself to start thinking about his time with Ella that night. It was nearly 5pm on his watch and she was collecting him at 7pm. Tadeusz felt as if he was back in a dream again. Was this really going to happen? How would she feel about him being old and grey? He had a sudden dread… What if they didn't find common ground other than what they had shared 30 years before? Tadeusz shook it off and ran a bath. He laid out his trousers to press. Then his jacket. And finally, his casual shirt. He planned not to wear a tie, for the first time in many years. He figured it would make him look a little younger although he was not confident about that concept. He smiled to himself again. It would be fine. He got into the hot bath and decided to re-read all of Ella's letters. Her words flowed. She had offered him so much love and affection. The feelings were unreserved. He stayed in the bath for over 40 minutes, indulging himself in the emotional words of his Ella.

By the time he had extracted himself from the bath and dried it was ten past six. His mouth was dry. She would be here soon. He started to dress but was still too hot from the bath. This was not the way he had planned, to be with only 30 minutes left for one of the most important appointments in his entire life. Eventually he calmed down and lit a cigarette to give himself a moment. All was now better. Tadeusz got up and donned his clothes. Tied his shoelaces and stretched up in front of the mirror to check himself. Did he look 24 again? No, he did not! He grimaced. He decided it had to do. He picked up his key and went down to reception.

CHAPTER 15

Ella had organised things so that she did not have to dress in front of her husband Witold. She asked him to work late at his office, which is what he did do on certain evenings anyway. So, he agreed to stay away and allow Ella her time to get ready. The last thing he wanted was to be there and watch his wife getting ready for another man. Especially a man who had stolen her heart before he had even met his Ella. He had shuddered at the prospect. But he had no choice. They had talked of this evening in a civilised way, but it was very soon made clear to him that there were no other options. Ella was going to meet Tadeusz and that was that. Ella, now a qualified judge, was a woman with her own mind, but rarely had she gone against Witold. She had let him run things at home. It was a relief not to be in charge of daily events. However, from the moment she had received Tadeusz's wonderful news of his planned journey to her, then all else fell by the wayside. Ella was going. She had gone shopping the day before to buy a special dress. One that she had not worn with Witold. She decided it was the right thing to do. Both for Witold but especially for Tadeusz. Ella chose a deep blue linen which was so very elegant and worked so well with her light grey hair. She was pleased with her choice and twirled in front of the mirror. Tadeusz would like this, she mused with a small smile. Ella added her perfume and applied minimal makeup. She felt she was ready for the most exciting date of her life. She felt 24 again. Ella went downstairs to the front door but stopped to leave a sweet note for Witold. He deserved that from her. All done, and Ella stepped out into the warm evening. She was almost with her Tadeusz. Embraced, in his arms, she hoped. Ella got into the car and drove the short distance to the Old Square. She had organised the same beautiful restaurant where he had proposed to her all of those

30 years ago. It would be so emotional, she pondered. And now within minutes Ella would see him again. Was this even possible? Would he be there? Perhaps there was a delay with flights? Or maybe he had changed his mind. These crazy thoughts flooded her mind as she walked towards the entrance to the rented apartment suites…

*

Ella was only around 100 metres from the double doors when she spotted Tadeusz standing outside. Tall and handsome in the evening sun. She knew him from almost any visible distance. Ella paused. After all of these years, there he stood. She was beyond any words. She sighed audibly and wanted to take in the man before her eyes. Her man. She started to walk with a brisk pace, when Tadeusz turned, and locked eyes with Ella. He smiled broadly and opened his arms as he started to walk towards her. Ella threw herself into his arms and hugged him as tightly as she could possibly muster. She held him and he held her, both holding on with a deep passion. Ella started to sob gently. She couldn't stop herself. He held her and whispered quietly that it was alright now. He told her that he was there for her. Despite his calming, tears were running down his cheeks. They both started to laugh gently. Both so happy to share this extraordinary moment. They refused to let go. Minutes passed and still they did not speak. They needed this embrace to reassure each other, that it was real and that they both felt the same way. Eventually Ella pulled back a little to allow herself to look into his face. She looked up adoringly. At his lines and crinkles around his eyes. To her he was still the handsome young graduate whom she had lost back then, before the war. And now he was alive in her arms. Ella was still too overcome to speak. She smiled again, reaching up to gently stroke his cheek. Tadeusz was quiet. He held Ella with his strong arms and absorbed every second that held them together. He looked back at his beautiful fiancée. And he found that she looked almost the same when she was such a beautiful young woman in 1939, the last time he saw her in Warszawa.

Eventually, Ella spoke first: 'My darling Tadeusz. You are still so handsome and not much has changed!' She laughed encouragingly.

'You have a few grey hairs, but your smile is still the same. I remember how it always captivated me.' And again she laughed.

Tadeusz stood there holding her close to him, and replied: 'And you, my darling, are as enchanting and beautiful as when I last saw you! Truly you look so breath-taking!' he exclaimed. And he hugged her back to his chest so tightly that she exhaled with a gentle giggle. Ella was so very excited that this meeting between them had happened in exactly the way she had hoped it would. Often, she had scolded herself for being too optimistic about how it might be.

Tadeusz and Ella had fallen in love as young graduates and had planned to marry. Now they were back in each other's arms. Both pondering what might have been had they been allowed to start a life together.

Tadeusz offered: 'So where shall we start? We have so much to talk about...'

Ella immediately replied: 'Let's not worry about how much time we have; we should go to our restaurant and just be. Together. We will find a way.' She smiled reassuringly.

So, they locked hands, quite naturally, and started to walk towards the restaurant across the square, both glancing at each other every few seconds. Nothing could come between them. It was as if they were back there in 1939, discussing their marriage plans. The same two people. The very same place.

Neither Tadeusz nor Ella had given a thought to either of their partners, Maria and Witold. They had been so lifted by their meeting, that they were in blissful harmony waiting to enjoy each other in a way that they had both frequently imagined these past months.

The Manager of the restaurant welcomed them with open arms, as he already knew a little of the background from Ella. He was thrilled to be part of this romantic reunion. The main table was by the window. Large, able to sit four people, but reserved exclusively for the two lovers. Tadeusz smiled and thanked the Manager for his generous spirit. Ella took off her coat and Tadeusz pulled back the chair for her to sit facing the restaurant. Tadeusz then took his chair, sat down and sighed. He looked at Ella as if to say how much he had been longing for this moment but had never believed that it would finally happen.

Ella looked deep into his eyes, searching for his next words. But they did not come. Tadeusz was still absorbing the moment that they had met and hugged. She reached across for his hand, which she held with both her hands across the table. He added his second hand so that they were locked together. Both looking at each other again, trying to understand how their lives had been shattered to pieces. And yet here they both were, almost 40 years on, as if nothing had indeed happened.

The waiter broke their silence, asking if they would like to order. Tadeusz looked at the waiter with a withering glance as if to say, 'come back tomorrow'. Ella laughed and suggested that perhaps they could get some wine to start and look at the menus so they could order. Tadeusz grudgingly concurred and then went back to holding hands and looking at his Ella. They ordered a bottle of Chablis, and then made their respective choices from the menu. Neither of them was too concerned about the food; they knew it would be wonderful whatever they picked. But more importantly they were about to start a conversation that had been put on hold for nearly half a century.

'So, my darling Tadeusz,' she said with tears in her eyes. 'Together in our country. In our city. At last we are able to speak together – face to face. I am faltering with my words as I cannot contain myself. Being here with you. I now feel totally complete. I don't much care what happens next as I have now shared my moment with you once more...' She looked down. Her shoulders were wracked with sobs. 'I know I have said all of this to you before, in my letters, but to discover that you were still alive...? That was the day when my world was turned upside down. How was that even possible? I had given up, but your spirit was always with me. Every day I went to work. Even when I got married, I smiled at you secretly. It was supposed to have been us. But I understood the ravages of war. You had died. And I was to move on with my life. Which I eventually did. With Witold. All of our dreams had finally disappeared. I started a new life, with a new husband and five sons. Yes, I was happy. But I had lost you and yet you never left me.'

Tadeusz watched her speaking. Looking into her

eyes. Feeling the pain she was expressing. His heart was pounding with heartache. He had really gone back in time and was now listening to his bride to be… the woman he had loved more than life itself. Ella was not asking for anything from him, but just wanted to tell him the journey she had taken through the years.

The food arrived. They stopped talking and sipped their soup, both deep in thought.

Tadeusz started first. 'Ella, my darling. I feel your pain so much. There was no way back to you, to my parents, to my old life. Nobody was allowed to return to Poland unless we were prepared to swear ourselves as die-hard communists. We heard terrible stories. We couldn't locate family or contact anybody inside Poland. Communications were forbidden.'

He paused as he was recovering his composure. Ella was holding his hand and she stretched out and touched his cheek, as if to say that she understood his traumas. She indeed had experienced her own versions of hell on earth with this man.

'I searched my heart to know what to say to you when we met. And I didn't know the answer. We spent so much time together back then. We were inseparable! And our plans were so clear. But now, after 30 years, there does not seem any way to wind back time. To start again. And yes, I am so in love with Maria. So how am I allowed to feel the way I do about you, my Ella? Yet I do! Can we love two people equally at the same time? Life's experience tells us that we cannot.'

He looked up at Ella. His eyes searching for some answers. Any words that would correct his thinking. He realised that he was speaking as a lost man. Despite all of his planned speeches, he was already at sea with his words.

Ella returned his gaze. She was moved by his softness and that his vulnerability showed so readily. This made him even more attractive to her, though that was not her intention. Ella believed that she had wanted this wonderful meeting to be her closure. For her and for him. But she had never held back her deep feelings. She was resolute and without limits in her search for their truth. Ella did not speak, as she wanted him to continue. Tadeusz could see that his last remark about loving both Maria and Ella had left her breathless. He really didn't know where to go next...

'It's an impossible situation for us, Ella. Here we are looking at our lives now and comparing to when we were here so many years ago, but tell me about you now.'

And he squeezed her hand. Ella sat back and gazed at him for a while. She really was not sure if she wanted to talk about career achievements. She liked the question about loving two people more… and wanted to explore that a little further.

'So, I can tell you that I do know that I love two men in my life. I am not sure that I can say that I love them equally. But I can say that I love them differently. The love I hold for you, Tadeusz, is exquisite. It is pure. It is for you, the person in my life who would never have an equal. My love for you was held by a young woman who had never loved before. The pain I felt when I believed you were lost was beyond words. The pain was so physical. I cannot begin to describe what I felt for the ten years after you left. And now you are here, in front of me. Am I different? Do I feel differently? And I can give you my honest answer that nothing has changed. From the second I received your first reply, I knew I could release the years of apprehensions inside me. I knew then that I could love you again, forever as I had loved you before.' Ella bowed her head. She had been leading up to say these words for a very long time. And now she had said them. Tadeusz was still. His head was dizzy. His feelings were a mess.

Just then, the waiters arrived with the main course. Tadeusz wondered if he could even begin to get through this course, knowing that it was his turn to speak since they were sharing thoughts back and forth across the table.

They looked at their food. But her words had cut deep. They were so honest and profound. Neither of them touched their utensils.

Tadeusz looked across at Ella. And simply said: 'I know. I have thought about this very point continuously for the past weeks while waiting for your letters. I discussed my trip with Maria and attempted to swear my undying love to her. I was trying to be clear that of course we loved each other. And I was merely going to see a very dear old friend whom I once knew and loved so very much. But at the time, Maria's expression told me that she knew differently. She understood so much better how these things work. She knew instinctively that I would come here and be entirely captivated by the woman I had promised to marry. And Maria was right. I am here, with you, and in a total daze. When I was waiting for your letters, I debated in my mind what I would say to you, with all sincerity and honesty. The truth is I really would have loved to have said what you just said to me. It was perfect. You captivated my entire heart with your words.'

He reached over again to clasp Ella's hand. They held hands and looked deeply into one another's eyes. They had said so much that should perhaps not have been said. They knew that they were both committed elsewhere. Yet they were stating that their feelings for each other were pretty much fundamental to their existence.

'I am so happy to hear your words, Tadeusz. It's so much more than I could possibly have hoped for. My only dream was that I could actually see you again. As I have said – you were dead! And then you were not! So, for me to find you, and be able to write to you, was already way beyond any aspirations that I had nurtured. Never did I think that you would come and see me. Here in our city. In our square. An impossibility. So, to have the opportunity to say these things to you is all I can dream of. Regardless of how you reply, I am now complete. I have told you of my love. Of the purity. And of the depths that I have reached to touch your soul.'

She leant back and smiled at him. Almost victoriously. Not in any kind of competitive way. But more as if to say that she had achieved all that any person in her position could have possibly wished for. Tadeusz smiled back at her, hopelessly lost in her beauty radiating across the table. He was clueless about what he could possibly say next. They were dangerously close to sounding as if they could start an affair, or were they indeed already having their affair?

Tadeusz leaned forward. 'What do you think our parents might be thinking right now?' he said, pointing up to the sky. 'I should imagine that they would be reeling in horror but secretly delighted.' They both hooted with laughter. It was a helpful release, as they were both completely immersed in the notion of what to do or say next.

'My parents would be thrilled. Perhaps they are thrilled. You know how much they loved you, Tadeusz?' she offered.

He smiled warmly and responded: 'Mmm. I think the same, as my parents loved you so much as well. Both our parents knew that ours was a match made in heaven. And we had planned to keep it that way.' He leaned back, frowning. They were straight back to their limitless love, so easily expressed to each other.

They both mused on these words. And sat looking at each other again. Ella blushed a little as her thoughts were on the fact that he was staying the night. Was this even possible? Was it terrible of her? How on earth could they take it to the next level? After all, she had already declared that she felt complete. Nothing else was required of him or anybody else. Ella had achieved the most wonderful desire of her life. To see Tadeusz just one more time. To touch his face and hold his hand. It was enough. She blushed again, as her head was asking – but just maybe…

Tadeusz was thinking that perhaps he might have gone too far. Had he let down his Maria? Or would she understand? She already knew that he would say these things. She knew him better than he knew himself.

So, he felt free to continue. He would make it up to Maria when he returned. He would not abandon his love for her… and then he noticed Ella slightly blushing and smiling to herself.

'So, my darling Ella. We have come so very far in these past weeks. So much further than that moment when I opened your first letter! Here we are talking to each other like lost lovers. Wondering why life had dealt as such a savage blow. Yet we found ourselves together again. Despite all the odds. Despite the years that have passed. We are together once more. And you look so beautiful tonight in the glow of the fire…' He looked down, slightly embarrassed as he knew he was now flirting with Ella. And so, did she know.

Ella reached for his hand again and looked into his eyes. 'Will this be our evening or is this our night?' And she looked down with a shy smile. Tadeusz's breath quickened. He was not sure that he was hearing the words correctly. Ella had just uttered words that were inconceivable to him, yet he knew that he had considered saying the same to Ella. But now this was perhaps a bridge too far. He yearned to take her in his arms. To make passionate love; the love that had been stolen from them both back then. But how could he face Maria when he returned? His head was a mess.

He looked up and Ella returned his gaze. He couldn't speak. He shook his head from side to side. It was not a rejection of the notion. He simply didn't know how to respond. They sat in silence, both considering the possibility and even more of the consequences.

Tadeusz sat still for some time and then turned to the waiter and asked for the bill. They continued to sit without a word. It seemed that they had crossed an invisible line and words could only damage their understanding.

CHAPTER 16

Tadeusz paid the bill and stood to help Ella with her chair. They both walked quietly to the entrance. The Manager was already walking alongside and asked: 'Was everything alright, sir?'

'Yes. Delightful,' said Tadeusz. 'We wanted to enjoy a stroll, so we decided to pass on the dessert.' He smiled gratefully at the Manager, and shook his hand, at the same time pressing some zloty notes into his hand.

The Manager bowed wisely and opened the door. 'Goodnight, sir and madame. We hope to see you both again very soon.'

They both stepped out into the cool air. Tadeusz put his arm gently around Ella's shoulders and pressed her to his side. She responded with a huge hug that made him chuckle. They walked slowly towards the river. They needed time to think, maybe talk a little more.

The river was close by. They found a path along which they could amble. Still they had not spoken since leaving the restaurant. Yet it all seemed so normal. As if they were a couple who had just enjoyed a special evening together. They stopped by the castle and turned towards each other. Tadeusz simply said: 'Let's go back to where I am staying and enjoy a nightcap together.' Ella nodded in agreement and turned to put her arm around his waist. They walked towards the apartments where they had met a few hours ago. So much had happened so quickly.

They arrived at the apartment block and Tadeusz used his key to get into the reception area. They went up in the lift and stood still in silence. Tadeusz opened his apartment door with the pass key and turned to Ella. 'What can I get you to drink, my darling?'

Ella smiled. 'A vodka would be nice,' she responded quietly.

Tadeusz turned to the drinks bar and made two

large vodkas with ice. His heart was racing. He couldn't control where this was going. He was with a woman he had once loved without limits. And now he was back with her here in Warszawa. Was it so unfair? He put his drink down and gently stepped towards Ella and lifted her from the sofa. She slipped into his arms with ease. She knew that this was the moment she had dreamed of most of her life. She laid her head on his chest as he held her tightly. He turned his head, and with his hand gently lifted her chin towards him. He kissed her softly at first. She yielded with a sigh. They kissed slowly, as if to submerge into themselves. Tadeusz pulled back slightly and, removed his jacket. She slipped her shawl off her shoulders, revealing her beautiful shoulders to his gaze. He nuzzled into her neck and then pulled his lips to her mouth. Now more hungrily and again she responded to match his urgency. They somehow managed to shuffle through to the bedroom, holding each other with mounting desire. They had both decided that this was right. After all of these years they had to consummate what had been stolen. It was only one night. It would seem so unreasonable if they stopped now.

They fell onto the bed, hugging and kissing. Tadeusz reached for the back of her dress and then suddenly stopped. His heart was pounding. He fell back onto the bed and stared at the ceiling. He couldn't do this to his Maria. Not after all that they had been through these past decades. He looked across at Ella who was staring at him as if in a state of total shock. She reached across and put her hand on his chest. She pulled to be closer and he embraced her with his arm. Ella kissed his neck gently. And Tadeusz turned back to her and kissed her again... He knew there was no way back. His longing and passion were both too strong. They continued to kiss. She felt his urgency pressing against her. Ella turned to undo her dress, but he stopped her. He wanted to do it himself. Slowly. He reached for the small zip and drew it down very carefully, all the time looking deeply into her eyes. She gasped with lust. She felt like a teenager, making love for the first time. Tadeusz could read her thoughts, as they matched his own. It was so clear to them both how they felt. He kissed her breasts, and began to make love to her body, all the time holding back with his final penetration. She lay back and shuddered with ecstasy. This was so completely beyond anything she had dreamed of and now her body was in a spasm of lust. With the man she had loved, deeply, from her teen years.

Tadeusz turned, and was now pulling her on top of him, ready to drive them both to heights beyond words. Ella responded, and slowly placed herself in position above him, all the time locking his eyes with her eyes. She gasped again, and soon they were in rhythmic abandon. It had only been some 20 minutes or so before they fell back, both smiling and even laughing a little with each other. A delirious moment for them both. They both were gently panting, still catching their breath. He reached over and drew Ella to his chest, where she rested her head. How extraordinary was this moment? They just smiled and stared at the ceiling. Both thinking. They could not have hoped for a more wonderful climax to their evening. Nothing mattered right there and then. Tomorrow was another day.

After an hour, Tadeusz awoke from his short slumber. Ella was not in his bed. Then he heard the shower and he knew that their time together had come to a close. His head hung in sadness. But his heart knew that they had enjoyed a perfect evening together. Now he had to draw that thought and moment to his heart and keep it there forever. He lay there wondering what was to come next. He had not a clue. And it was 2am. Ella came through in her dressing gown. She smiled warmly but had small tears in her eyes.

'It's my time, my darling. Witold will be wondering where I might be. I did say that I would be late. But this is very late.' She smiled again. Tadeusz reached out to her, and she tumbled into his arms. He gently kissed the top of her head and then he reached down to her lips. They kissed passionately again. The hunger rose but this time more slowly. Both wanted the moments to last for a long time in their hearts. Tadeusz undid her gown and touched her softly between her legs. She shuddered with lust, but so much mixed with her love for this man who was to have been her husband for life. He drew her down on top of him, all the time looking into her soft eyes, smiling touched with tears of joy. She gasped when he entered her again and they moved slowly together both enthralled with each other's gentle passion. She pushed hard against him, driving as deep as she could go. As if to own him forever, or at least leave him marked for life. Tadeusz groaned as they moved a little faster. He was lost to her. In complete unison, they came together, something he had not experienced for some years. He embraced Ella and hugged her closely, knowing that the time was soon to come to let her go... they held hoping that neither would let go. Ella leant back after some time and said:

'Now I must go. Before I stay forever!' She giggled nervously, thinking how true a statement that was in her mind.

Tadeusz frowned and nearly said the words that she needed to hear. But he stopped himself. He again stroked her cheek and she pulled away to start to get dressed. Tadeusz watched his beautiful woman finishing the last touches to her clothes and makeup. She had to leave looking exactly as she had at the start of the evening. But the expression in her eyes told a very different story.

Tadeusz got up and quickly dressed as well. He wanted to walk her to her car. He was desperate not to let her go too soon. The seconds were hurtling past them at speed. Finally, she looked at him, and embraced him with all of her strength. Tadeusz squeezed back. They both could hardly breathe. They released and she walked to the door. Tadeusz followed her. He left his luggage in the room and followed her down the one flight of stairs to the main door entrance. She turned to embrace his side with her arm while he put his around her shoulders. They walked in silence. The car stood there in the distance. Only a hundred metres left to go.

Eventually they arrived at the car. Tadeusz turned to tell her how much he loved her; how hard he was going to find the next minutes, the next years. How he thought of staying forever. But Ella stopped him. She put her finger to his lips and shook her head gently.

'Let's not speak. Let's cherish this moment forever. And what will be will be.' She reached up to his lips and said: 'Au revoir, my darling beloved Tadeusz.'

And with that she opened the door, jumped in and drove off without looking back. Tadeusz was decimated. Shattered. He couldn't move. Ella was already gone. With him one minute, and then gone, seemingly forever.

He stood there for what seem an eternity, deep in his thoughts. He lit his second cigarette and turned and slowly walked towards the apartment block in the Old Square. He stood at the main door and took in the beauty of this miracle of architectural recovery after the German bombings. He thought back to his time here when he had just graduated. He looked at the bars where he and Ella had shared a drink or two, with local friends. All with their own particular dreams of the future.

He sighed and thought again about his evening with Ella. His plans of what to say and what to share had been completely abandoned. He had thrown away all his caution. He had connected with Ella on every level of passion without limitation. He had reached a very strange crossroad in his life.

He climbed the stairs heavily. Tadeusz packed his clothes. He had a shower, reluctant to wash away the smells of his beloved Ella. Eventually he emerged in his robe. Took out another cigarette and sat on the bed. Some hours later he awoke with a start. He checked his watch, which showed 9.30am. Thankfully he had slept for a few hours. His flight was at 12.30pm so he got up and put together his overnight case.

When he got to the airport, Tadeusz called Maria, as he knew she would be waiting, and the absence of a call would make things much worse.

'Hi, my darling,' he said enthusiastically. 'Am on my way home; back soon!'

'Oh, good,' she replied. 'How was your evening?' she asked.

'Well it was really enjoyable. Slightly strange as we had not seen each other for over 35 years so to be expected. But then we got talking and we both warmed up...'

'Warmed up?' Maria laughed nervously. She was not really in the mood to talk now. Maria wanted to see his face to judge what had happened.

'No. No! Just we got rid of the awkwardness and then we talked about the old times. As that is all we had together. The past, back then. Anyway, I will tell you all when I see you. I should be back in Bournemouth by 6pm. I checked the train connections and that's the time estimated for arrival.'

'OK. Well, safe travels. I will have a nice supper

ready for us when you get back. Hugs, my darling,' she said.

'And to you.' And with that they both ended the call.

He had not had any time to decide exactly what he would say. The short conversation had already forced him to cover his evening tracks without revealing anything about what had happened. His head was dizzy with shock. The reality was so very different to what he had told Maria. Now he really had to think carefully what he would say when he got back.

Tadeusz glided through the airport deep in thought. He could hardly answer any questions at passport control and continued to the departure gate in a mild daze. So, what was he going to say? He considered the options, all the time thinking of his time with Ella. He was in serious state of confusion. He had really not expected anything like this. He had not considered this situation, and therefore had no idea what he really would say. Slowly he started to unravel his feelings.

He knew that he loved Ella and would love her for the rest of his life. That was certain in his mind.

Maria? He loved her and had been in love with her through their entire marriage. Maria was the core, the strength of their joint existence. Maria represented all that he ever wanted from his partner. They were a complete couple, both loving each other year after year of their lives together. All of that was a simple fact. And at no stage had Tadeusz ever wanted to even think about dismantling any part of that magic they had shared all of these years.

But his life had been sliced open by Ella, the woman he had promised to marry a very long time ago. He had consummated that promise last night with so deep a passion that it shocked him to his very core.

The flight was on time and soon he landed back in the UK. His extraordinary 24 hours had passed. It was now behind him and he was returning to his normal life with Maria. In some ways he was almost relieved as the heights he had reached with Ella could not be sustained in any possible shape. He did want his life back with his partner Maria. He really yearned to get home now and wanted to get past their conversation about his trip. He wanted that next morning when they would have breakfast, a black coffee and move along together effortlessly in their daily lives.

However, he first had to get through tonight. He had given up trying to second guess the conversation he was due to have with Maria. He arrived back in Bournemouth at around 6.45pm. The taxi dropped him at the top of the long drive. He got out and strode down the path hesitatingly but also with determination.

He put the key in the door, and Maria opened it for him. He dropped his case and drew her to him with a huge hug. She pressed back against him, returning the hug with equal force. She pulled back and looked up at him. He was grinning widely and kissed her on the lips, again squeezing her to him.

'It's so very good to have you back, although perhaps a little strange.'

'Why strange?' he asked, looking at her face for clues.

'Oh, nothing much. Just it's unusual to welcome back your husband from a trip abroad when he has been back to visit with his ex-fiancée!' she laughed, trying to lighten the observation.

'Well, yes, I can see that,' he said lightly, all the

time being cautious with any responses. Maria did know him better than he knew himself. He had long ago admitted that women understood things much better than men, and Maria was at the top of that 'understanding' league.

They walked down the corridor arm in arm. Tadeusz could see that their dining table had been laid, and with a candle. He loved the small detail. He believed that it showed that Maria wanted a warm and loving evening, and not a confrontation. He told her that he would freshen up and join her in a few minutes. Maria smiled, acknowledging his movement to the bathroom and turned to the kitchen to complete the cooking. She had prepared his favourite. A Viennese schnitzel with roasted potatoes and a light salad. After about 15 minutes Tadeusz emerged holding a small package. A present he had purchased in the Old Square just before finding his apartment block. It was a silver brooch with a beautiful amber stone setting. Very traditionally Polish. Maria opened the present and gasped.

'My darling, you should not have but it is truly beautiful. And from our homeland. So special. Thank you so much, Tadeusz.' She reached up and stroked his check and added a quick kiss on the lips. He responded with a small hug. He loved how Maria was always so appreciative of any small gifts that he might give her. He liked to buy her the odd present.

'I'm glad you like it. You know I'm not too good with jewellery,' he laughed. And they hugged again.

Maria told him to sit. She poured them both a glass of red and turned to the oven.

Tadeusz knew that this must not turn into any kind of inquisition, even a veiled one. It had to be a natural conversation. He knew he had decided not to share the last moments of his evening with Ella. His love for Maria was as strong as it had been before his time in Warszawa and even before the time when the first letter arrived. He dearly wanted to answer the questions and get past this conversation.

Maria laid out the food on their two plates. She sat down and lifted her glass, to which Tadeusz said, 'Cheers. I'm so glad to be back home with you.' And he really meant it.

'Thank you, my darling. Cheers to you too and it's lovely to have you back,' she replied. 'So, tell me about your trip. But Tadeusz, let me first say to you, please don't feel you have to tell me about any intimate words you might have shared. I don't need to hear them. You are back and that is enough for me...'

Maria had delivered an extraordinary statement. And certainly, one that he had really not expected. Not at all. Tadeusz looked at her and wondered if she knew. How much did she know? He certainly knew that he should never underestimate Maria. Not under any circumstances. And he also understood that Maria would have thought carefully about that opening gambit. So how should he reply? He started his food to gain a few seconds before he replied.

'Thank you for that. It's really generous of you. Our evening did have its moments of expression. The setting was beautiful in the Old Square. We should go back there soon so you can also visit our old country. We ate at an old established restaurant Ella had booked. The food was delicious.' He paused. Maria smiled.

'That sounds lovely. And yes, I would love to go back there with you one day soon. But how was your conversation without the absolute detail? Did you both consider running away together or did you simply exchange notes on both of your respective lives?' Maria giggled nervously but also with a slight steely glint in her eye.

Tadeusz knew that this was the moment he had to hold his nerve. He so wanted to return to the old life he had shared with Maria. And in that very moment, he realised that if he told her of the encounter with Ella, he would lose Maria forever. He knew that Maria might even know what happened, using her amazing instincts, but they could not share the knowledge openly. Not now. Not ever.

Tadeusz looked up and said: 'It was an amazing evening, Maria. I met with someone whom I loved very much many years ago. Our meeting was extraordinary. We were able to share so much of what was back then. We went over the times and the people we knew then. About those who had survived. About our respective parents. And now I am here back with you, the woman I have always loved with all my heart and will always love until the day I die.' He looked directly at her and she back at him.

They stared at each other for what seemed an endless age. Maria had tears in her eyes. And Tadeusz was starting to well up at the sight of her tears. Maria got up and walked around the table; Tadeusz quickly got up and they both rushed into an embrace. They both hugged and hugged. Both knew that there was nothing more that could be said, nor should be said. The words were clear, and they contained what Maria wanted from him. An expression of undying love to the end of their days. She decided that she would live with the slight uncertainty and she knew that in time she would get over that unanswered question.

They sat down together and continued to eat quietly. They sipped their wine and smiled. After a while Maria talked about the hotel and the various clients that had stayed. Tadeusz always enjoyed Maria's version of the guests as she really knew how to read them individually and was almost always right. Maria knew what was thought and felt without the words being spoken. Her instincts were as good as it gets.

At the end of the evening, they retired to bed. Maria knew not to provoke any love making. She did not need to make any claim on him. It was not a territorial game. Tadeusz was back and he belonged to her. She knew that.

CHAPTER 17

Tadeusz woke the morning feeling weirdly happy. His evening with Ella was entirely intact in his mind. Every single second of their time together right up to the moment when she drove away at 2am. Yet he was so content to be back as he felt safe with his Maria. This was his home and this was his woman. And he would never mess with that again. He decided to write Ella one last letter as they both deserved that.

He retired to his study as usual after breakfast. Maria had been friendly and affectionate. But also occupied with the hotel chores. They kissed and he left her in the kitchen talking to the maid, Joana.

He took out some paper and thought. He was not worried about Maria coming in as he knew she would not want to see any words he might scribe. She would know that he would write once more.

My dearest darling Ella,

I am still in a daze. Our time together was more magical than words can express. Every single second was special. It was so very wonderful to see you looking so beautiful after all these years. And for me to have those hours with you in the restaurant was so enchanting. I did have high expectations for our meeting but all of those were easily surpassed. I just loved being there with you. And speaking with you. And laughing with you.

Then when I believed that our evening was at its highest point, you gently blushed. And I was lost in your eyes. Later I was lost in you for what seemed like an eternity and then turned into a moment.

I look back on that wonderful evening with you and can feel every single second inside my head and heart. I know you felt the same way and that we will share forever together.

I returned to Maria and I was honest with her about our affection and conversations. I am glad to say that she did not probe any further and actually suggested that she did not want any of the intimate details of our time together. For me that was so special on her part as it allows me to hold you dear in my heart forever without bearing any guilt of that time. So, our time and our memory remains pure in me and I hope in you.

I am very much in love with Maria. And she will be my bride for the rest of our days together. I needed to say that to you, even though I know you already know that. I have concluded that one can love two people at the same time. Maybe differently but yes both immensely.

That leads to me to this painful moment. I have decided that we cannot continue to correspond. It would be wrong and inappropriate. The moments we have been able to grasp back from time, are ours and always will be.

The future has to be that we return to our loved ones and no longer damage that with our continued letters. It hurts me deeply to ask you not to write again. But we both know that it would continue to cause havoc and mayhem with our emotions. With our affections. With our love.

I have to say now goodbye, my darling. I thank you from the bottom of my heart for finding me. For pursuing me. And for sharing yourself with me. I will never forget you my darling Ella. Never.

Your Tadeusz

He did not have the courage to re-read the letter. He put his head in his hands and thought for some time. The letter lying there in front of him. After an hour or so he took the last letter. He put a stamp on the addressed envelope. And he walked off to the letterbox at the top of their street. Finally, he pushed it into the slot. On its way to his Ella.

Please do not reply, my darling Ella, he thought... *Please don't.*

Ella picked up her pen and started:
My Darling and Beloved Tadeusz...

THE END

AUTHOR'S NOTE

Maybe.

ABOUT THE AUTHOR

Matthew Lutostanski is 75. He wrote this, his first book, during the COVID pandemic. Like most people who have a first book roaming in their soul, Matthew sought out time and passion to develop a story which had been in his mind for some time. Matthew is already starting his second novel.

Printed in Great Britain
by Amazon